A GRIM GAME

BLYTHE BAKER

Secrets unraveled...

When Rose Beckingham is hired to investigate a baffling museum robbery, the case leads her into a trap set by her nemesis, the Chess Master. While working to ensnare the mysterious villain once and for all, Rose must finally confront the lies of her own past.

Drawn into a dangerous game by the most elusive criminal in London, Rose risks everything to track down her enemy before time runs out. But with her quarry about to escape, taking all the answers with him, will Rose and Achilles unravel the final truth before it slips out of reach forever?

1

The morning was drenched in gray. Rain squelched from the heavy sky like it was being wrung out over the city and fallen leaves mildewed along the streets and sidewalks. Everyone who found themselves out in the dreary day kept their heads down, hats pulled low over their eyes, shoulders hunched near their ears. It felt like the perfect day to visit prison.

I'd debated a long while about whether I wanted to visit my cousin Edward in prison or not. He was set to stand trial for the murder of Mr. Matcham, along with a charge of attempted murder for when he tried to kill me, as well. The last time I'd seen my cousin, he'd fired his gun at me and chased me halfway across his family's large property in Somerset before being accidentally shot himself. So, given the circumstances, my desire to see him again was minimal. My curiosity, however, drove me to make the trip.

Before he attempted to murder me, Edward had made his confession. He'd told me that he contacted a powerful man in London's criminal underworld to obtain the lethal and rare poison he'd used to kill Mr. Matcham. I had reason to believe the man Edward spoke of was the same man who had written me prior to Mr. Matcham's demise to warn me of a death in the countryside. The man I had come to refer to as the "Chess Master" due to his penchant for leaving chess pieces along with his notes. And after his latest delivery of the most powerful chess piece on the board, the King, I could no longer keep my burning questions to myself. Edward had seen the Chess Master's face. He had done business with him before, and I knew he could tell me the mysterious man's true identity.

The Surrey House of Correction, where Edward had been moved since recovering from his gunshot wound, was a good distance from my home. While I had my own personal driver, George, I didn't want him to know of my plan. He wouldn't have been able to stop me from visiting Edward, even though he would have wanted to, but still, I wanted to go alone. I didn't want to have to explain to anyone why I was visiting my attempted murderer. And I especially didn't want to have to explain it to the rest of Edward's family. So, I took a cab and instructed the driver to drop me off a distance from the prison, opting to walk the rest of the way. The Beckingham family was understandably shocked and appalled by Edward's actions, and as the trial loomed, they were trying to keep a low profile. The last thing they needed was for news of my visit to reach the papers—*Edward Beckingham's Victim Turned Visitor*.

There had been enough articles in the last few weeks about the "divide" Edward's crimes had caused. Not only had he murdered his sister's secret lover—an affair which was no longer secret—but he had attempted to murder me, his own cousin. Reporters claimed to have the inside story, explaining that I was at odds with the Beckinghams, and that they would never forgive me for taking the witness stand to testify against their son and brother.

None of it was true, of course. True, Catherine had come to me and asked that I consider not testifying against Edward, and Lord Ashton had been reluctant to accept that Edward could truly be responsible for the crimes he was charged with. But, as time had gone on and the investigation came to a close, the truth had come out, and no one could deny Edward's guilt. After weeks of not seeing the Beckinghams, I'd received an invitation to dinner, which I'd readily and nervously accepted. There, the family had sought to make amends.

"We are so glad you accepted our invitation," Lady Ashton said, reaching out to grab my hand and squeeze my fingers. "We all missed you, Rose."

I smiled at my aunt and then cautiously glanced around the table. Alice was nodding in eager agreement with her mother, and I was relieved to see that Catherine and Lord Ashton were nodding, as well.

"I missed you, as well. All of you," I said, giving Catherine a pointed look. She smiled.

Lord Ashton coughed, his fist over his mouth, and then began to speak. "When all of this came to light, things were confusing. We didn't have all the information, and it was impossible to think a family member we all loved could be capable of such a horrific act. In our desire to clear Edward of blame, I know it may have felt as though some that blame landed on you, Rose."

I shook my head, trying to stop Lord Ashton's apology in its tracks. I had been hurt by his anger towards me at first, but soon I came to realize from where the feelings stemmed. It was easier to blame me than to think he had raised a murderer. And while it wasn't fair, I understood. I didn't

blame him for anything he'd said or done in those
confusing days.

"No, it's important that this is spoken aloud and made
known. We are all sorry for any additional pain we may
have caused you, Rose. As the truth has been revealed, we
have come to accept Edward's responsibility. And in doing
so, have been ashamed by how you were treated and abandoned in the early days of the investigation."

Lady Ashton hiccupped, and I looked over to realize she
was crying. I patted her shoulder, and she covered my hand
with her own, her lips pursed in a sad smile.

Lord Ashton continued. "You are a prized member of
this family, Rose. Edward sought to harm you because of his
own guilt, and he has brought shame on our family. His
crimes will forever be a blight on our honor. But you, dear
Rose, represent the best the Beckinghams have to offer. We
asked you here to dinner, so we could formally apologize to
you for our behavior in the days and weeks after the
murder."

While the declaration had been awkward and left me
nearly speechless, it was nice to hear, nonetheless. The
Beckinghams were the closest thing to family I had left—I
highly suspected Lord Ashton would not have made such an
apology to me if he knew I was not truly Rose Beckingham,
but actually her former servant in disguise—and I wasn't
eager to lose them anytime soon.

Still, even with the apology, it was difficult to be
around the family of late. While they had forgiven me,
they still struggled to accept Edward's new identity as a
murderer, and my presence and the impending trial did
little to help them forget. I did my best to keep my
distance and offer them privacy to mourn and come to
terms with their new reality. And that meant I had no

intention of telling them about the visit I was paying to Edward in prison.

The sun was rising behind the massive brick building, casting it into deep shadow. It looked like a blot on the horizon—a black ink stain across a perfectly clean sheet of paper that should be crumpled up and forgotten. Even looking at the building from the outside was a dreary exercise, so I didn't particularly wish to experience the inside. However, that would be the only way to speak with Edward.

The guards at the gate were reluctant to let me inside, but the men inside were even more difficult to convince. One of them, a balding man with a thick mustache and dirty suspenders, crossed his arms where he stood behind a cluttered desk and shook his head when I asked to see Edward Beckingham.

"He's on trial for murder. Only family allowed," he barked, dismissing me with a wave of his hand.

"I am family," I said.

He raised an eyebrow. "You a sister or something?"

"Or something." I didn't want word of my visit to make it back to the Beckinghams, and I didn't want anyone to look at me the way so many people were looking at me lately, with pity in their eyes. I had survived and I had my freedom. As far as I was concerned, I was not a victim, though it was difficult to convince everyone else of that.

The man shifted his weight from side to side, stretching his shoulders out wide. "You can't see him unless you are blood family."

I sighed. "I'm his cousin."

He narrowed his eyes at me. I could see the ghost of recognition in his face. "Cousin?"

"Do you know anything about this case?" I asked.

The man nodded his head slowly, clearly suspicious of

me. I couldn't exactly blame him. He probably didn't see many young women knocking on the prison doors before sunrise, a hat and scarf pulled around their face to avoid detection.

I unwound the thick scarf from around my neck and draped it over my arm. "I'm Edward's cousin. *The* cousin."

His overgrown brow furrowed for a second and then jolted upward in surprise. He shook his head as he pushed the door open and let me inside. "That makes you family, all right."

I was directed to a small concrete room to wait. It smelled wet and stale, and I found it difficult to inhale. For a moment, I felt a twinge of sympathy for Edward. He was accustomed to a much more luxurious life than what prison offered. And just as quickly as my sympathy came on, it passed. Edward was a murderer. A man who would have murdered again to save his own hide.

Just as I had this revelation, the door opened and a pale, thin creature was thrown in the room with me. It took several seconds for me to recognize my cousin. In the weeks he'd been in prison, his face had hollowed, his tan skin had turned an ashen gray color, and the thick dark locks of his hair had gone dry and brittle. Still, there was a familiar spark in his eyes, a haughtiness that couldn't be tempered by incarceration.

"Hello, Rose," Edward said, tipping his head to the side as if he needed to see me from another angle to be certain it was me.

"Edward." I tried to keep my voice level, unemotional. If I showed any weakness, he would latch onto it. I had to be unaffected if I wanted to gather any information from him.

He lowered himself into the wooden chair across from mine, moving slower than I'd ever seen him move, though he had the same graceful air. "I didn't expect to see you until the trial."

"I didn't expect to come," I admitted.

"And why did you?" he asked, leaning back, hands folded over his chest. It was then I noticed the metal cuffs around his wrists, the chain that bound them together. It was a comforting reminder. He could not hurt me here. Just outside the door was a guard who would burst into the room at the first sign of trouble. "Surely, you've been told not to fraternize with me. I suspect you'll be testifying against me in the trial."

It was a statement more than a question, but regardless, I had no intention of responding to it.

"I'm not here about the trial, and I don't intend to discuss it with you. The decision regarding my testimony is my own." I paused, leveling my gaze at him so he would know I was serious. Then, I continued. "I'm here to ask you a question."

Edward's dark eyebrows rose slowly. "Ask whatever you'd like, dear cousin. I cannot promise an answer, but I can promise to listen."

Dear cousin. The words sounded slimy rolling off his tongue, and suddenly I wanted to take back the entire idea. Instead of sitting across from Edward in prison, I wanted to be warm beneath the blankets of my bed at home. I swallowed back my rising nausea and looked Edward square in the face.

"You mentioned the shadowy figure who supplied the poison you used to end Mr. Matcham's life," I said, easing into the question.

Edward shook his head. "I said no such thing."

I furrowed my brow, confused. And then Edward winked, and I realized what was going on. He wouldn't be heard by anyone—me or the guard—admitting to his crimes.

"You mentioned a member of the criminal underworld," I said, rephrasing the question. "Would you tell me his name?"

"Why are you interested in associating with a criminal?" he asked. "I thought you were the solver of crimes, not the purveyor of them."

The truth was, I didn't want to seek out the Chess Master at all. I wanted to forget about him and move on from the entire incident. However, I'd asked Detective Achilles Prideaux to look into the whereabouts of my long-lost brother Jimmy—though Achilles did not know our familial connection—and he hadn't had any luck. Whereas, the Chess Master had supplied me with solid evidence that he had some connection to Jimmy, though I had no idea how strong it was. He was the only person who had given me any hope of finding my brother, yet I had no clue as to his identity. Unfortunately, the Chess Master knew my secret identity. He knew I was not truly Rose Beckingham but actually Nellie Dennet, and I knew he could choose to share this information anytime he wanted. It felt as though an invisible sword was held just above my head, and with every passing day, the blade lowered. I had to find the Chess Master as soon as possible.

And as it stood, Edward was the only person I knew who could connect me to the Chess Master, and the Chess Master was the only person I knew who could connect me to Jimmy. Essentially, Edward was my only hope.

I knew, however, that I couldn't tell any of this to Edward. He was in a precarious legal situation, no doubt facing terrible punishment should he be convicted of murder, and my testimony would almost certainly convict him. If he knew how desperately I needed this information, he would definitely try to use it as a bargaining chip, and then the only way I'd get anything out of him would be to choose not to testify or to lie on the witness stand.

I said, "The man has sought me out on several occasions but has kept his identity a secret from me. I would like to know to whom I have been talking."

"He contacted you?" Edward asked, dubious. "Why would he do that?"

"It is not important," I said firmly. "Can you help me uncover his identity or not?"

Edward lifted his chin, looking down his nose at me. "Of course, I can. The question is whether I will or not."

I sighed and stood to leave. "This is ridiculous. I am not here to play games with you, Edward."

"You aren't going anywhere," Edward said with a laugh.

He was right. He'd called my bluff. I had no intention of leaving the cold, damp room until I had an answer one way or the other from him.

"You may be surprised to hear this, Rose, but the men in here are not excellent company. So, you'll have to excuse me if I drag this meeting out awhile longer."

"Why do you want to talk to me?" I asked. "You tried to kill me, remember?"

Edward shook his head, a small smile on his lips. "I did no such thing. Though, if I had, it surely would have been out of necessity and not because of any ill will towards you."

A shiver ran down my spine. Why hadn't I ever noticed Edward's cool manners? The way he spoke around the truth, dangled the true meaning of his words in front of you like a treat and then yanked them back? He was diabolical. Though, I reminded myself, he was also in prison. He'd been fooled once—by me, in fact—and he could be fooled again. As always, he believed himself to be the cleverest person in the room, but one of us could leave the cage, the other couldn't. Clearly, I had the upper hand.

"Actually, I will leave. I don't want the information badly enough to endure this horrid place," I said, pushing my chair back and smoothing out the chiffon fabric of my dress. "I'll be sure to send my regards with your family, whenever they are able to make it out for another visit. If not, I'm sure I'll see you in the courtroom."

Edward's face was expressionless and stony as I left the table, but by the time I was halfway to the door, he cracked.

"Wait," he said, swiveling in his chair, the chains around his wrists clanking on the table. "I will give you answers."

I stopped, one foot lifted mid-step, and looked over my shoulder. "I told you. I don't want answers badly enough to spend any more time here. You want to toy with me, Edward, and I'm not interested."

"The roof leaks in my cell," Edward said, his voice quiet, wavering around the words. "It's cold and damp. Men die in here because of the conditions. I've felt ill for weeks. Even if they don't execute me, I'll die in this place."

I turned to face him, my arms hanging loosely at my sides. I had never seen Edward look so vulnerable. Still, I didn't want to give him even the tiniest hint that I felt for him.

He lowered his face, staring down at his feet, and continued. "I wanted to protect my sister's honor—my family's honor—but instead I have besmirched it irreparably. The only thing I ask is that you all do not forget me."

His words echoed off the hard walls until everything aside from our breathing went quiet. Then, a metallic bang rang out, and I instinctively ducked.

"Visit over," the guard outside the door barked, not even bothering to form a full sentence.

Edward looked up at me, eyes wide, stricken. "Come back," he demanded. "Come see me again, and I'll tell you whatever you want to know."

The guard banged on the metal door again, and I moved towards him, my ears ringing.

"Please, Rose," Edward called, outright begging now. "Come see me again. I'll help you with whatever you need. Please."

The guard opened the door for me and I stepped into the hall. Just before the door closed, I gave Edward one small nod. His face broke into a hopeful smile, and then the door slammed closed, and he was gone.

2

Aseem was bringing food out from the kitchen when I returned, setting the table for lunch.

"How did you know I'd be home in time to eat?" I asked as I unraveled my scarf and threw it over a hook next to the door.

"I hoped," Aseem said, laying the last plate of bread in the center of the table, folding his hands in front of him, and stepping away.

He'd been a small child when I'd found him hiding below deck on the RMS Star of India. It had only been a few months since then, but he had grown tremendously. His thin arms and legs had muscled and his soft jawline had squared off, but he moved with the same quiet grace he'd always had.

He left as I sat down to eat, and I could hear him moving around in the kitchen. It had been a good idea to hire him to serve in my house. He allowed me my privacy and knew how to anticipate my needs. The only problem was urging him to take a break from time to time. George, on the other hand, didn't need to be convinced. I gave him two days per week off and he accepted them without hesitation, keeping to himself and disappearing into the separate house where he lived out back.

I didn't realize how hungry I was until I began to eat. I'd skipped breakfast in order to get to the prison early. Afterwards, I'd wandered the city streets until my feet couldn't carry me any further, thinking about Edward's offer. I'd promised him I'd come back to the prison, but it felt like a bad idea. His complaints about prison sounded sincere, and I had no reason to doubt it was every bit as horrible as he said, but I also knew Edward. There had to be an ulterior motive to asking me back. And if I did go back, how could I be sure he'd give me the information I wanted? Would it be another waste of time?

The walk had done little to clear my head and questions were still clouding my brain when there was a knock at the door. Before I could even push myself away from the table, Aseem walked brusquely through the dining room.

"I'll answer it, Miss Rose."

I heard voices at the door for a moment, and then nothing. The door closed and Aseem appeared. His hands were folded behind his back, his dark face pale and blotchy. He looked as though he had seen a ghost.

"Who was at the door, Aseem?" I asked, standing from my chair. "Is everything all right?"

He opened his mouth and then closed it, taking a deep breath. "I'm not entirely sure, Miss. Perhaps, you should sit down."

"I'm all right," I said, waving away his concern. "Out with it. Tell me what is going on."

He nodded and held out the letter he'd been holding behind his back. "Officers were at the door. They left this letter for you."

"Officers? Did they need to see me? Is this about Edward and what happened in Somerset?" I asked. It was unlike Aseem to be so withholding. Usually, he spoke with absolute clarity. I wished he'd return to that method, because I was growing very impatient.

"They only left the letter. I haven't read it, but one of the officers informed me of the contents."

I grabbed the letter from Aseem and tore open the wax sealed envelope. It was from the Surrey House of Correction. "What did they say?" I asked, though my eyes were already skimming over the scratchily written message.

Aseem spoke at the same time I came to the point of the letter. "Your cousin Edward has died, Miss."

I fell back down into my chair, the wind pressing out of my lungs. I shook my head, read through the letter from the prison physician a second time, and then shook my head again.

"I just saw Edward," I said, though it came out sounding like a question. "This morning. I saw him this morning. A few hours ago."

"You were at the prison, Miss?" Aseem asked.

I nodded. "I went to see him, and he was fine."

That wasn't entirely true. His cheeks had been sunken in, his eyes tired and bloodshot. He'd looked better, but I hadn't been concerned for his health. And now, he was dead.

"The officers had just come from your aunt and uncle's house," Aseem said softly.

I jumped up from my chair. "Of course, how selfish. I should go to them. Call for George, please."

Leaving most of my lunch unfinished, I folded the letter and tucked it into my bag, and then went out front to wait for George. He came to a stop along the curb and jumped out to open my car door.

"You received word that Edward Beckingham has died, Miss?" George asked.

"Yes, he has. I must get to the Beckinghams immediately," I said.

George offered me a hand to help me into the back seat, and it wasn't until he was behind the wheel that I, once again, realized how selfish I'd been.

"I'm so sorry, George. You worked for the Beckinghams for a long time. I'm sure you knew Edward well."

He nodded. "I thought I did. Though, with the latest news coming out about him, I'm not sure any of us knew him half as well as we thought."

I hummed in agreement.

"Of course," George continued. "This is a tragedy, nonetheless."

"Indeed," I said, still hardly believing it could be true.

When we arrived at Ashton House, George offered to escort me inside, but I declined, to which he looked eternally relieved. George had worked for the Beckinghams for many years, but when they became aware of a few criminal incidents in his past that he had failed to disclose when he was hired, they relieved him of his duties. I didn't think now would be an appropriate time for a reunion. In fact, I wasn't even certain if I should be barging in on them. Surely, they would all be beside themselves with grief. I felt numb with shock, but Edward was their son and brother. Their pain would be unimaginable.

I knocked on the door and waited, but when no one answered after a few minutes, I cracked the door and stepped inside. I decided the servants must have been ordered not to answer the door these days. The family must be getting a lot of unwanted visitors with all the publicity lately. The entrance hall was dark, the doors leading into the sitting room and dining room closed. All of the shutters were drawn, and it felt as though the house had been closed up for years, abandoned.

"Hello?" I called quietly, my voice echoing off the walls. I strained to hear a sound, even the faintest footstep in the belly of the house, but there was nothing. Perhaps all of the family had gone to the prison. Maybe they had to claim Edward's body.

Body. Edward was a body. The thought sent a shiver down my spine. Him lying on a cold table, a sheet pulled over his face. How had he died? The letter had been nondescript, mentioning only that he had been declared dead. In truth, I'd come to the Beckingham's home in part because I hoped they had more thorough information than I did.

I toyed with the idea of stepping into the sitting room, but it was clear no one was at home, and I didn't want to intrude. So, I quietly turned and was halfway to the door when the sitting room doors burst open.

"Oh, Rose!"

I jolted forward, barely catching myself on the front door. Before I could turn around, arms were thrown around my waist, a head of long brown hair tucked into my side.

"Alice," I breathed, my heart rate slowly returning to normal. "It's you."

I placed a hand on her back and realized her shoulders were shaking. Then, I heard the sobs.

"Oh, Alice," I said, bending forward, covering her with my body. "I'm so sorry. So incredibly sorry."

Alice was still wrapped around me when Lady Ashton appeared in the doorway. Her face was splotchy, eyes swollen shut with tears.

"You came," she croaked out, arms open for a hug, though I couldn't move with Alice fixed to my side.

"As soon as I heard," I said.

When we made it to the sitting room, I saw Lord Ashton standing near a window as though he were looking out on the street, though that was impossible since the shades were drawn. Catherine was splayed across a sofa. Neither of them showed any outward sign that they had noticed my appearance at all.

"How are you?" I asked, directing the question to Lady Ashton. It felt like a silly thing to say, but then again, most things are silly when someone you love has just died. And all things are silly when that person was also a murderer. I had a strong feeling I was treading in very unfamiliar waters. There was no common etiquette for this particular circumstance.

"Devastated," Lady Ashton said, keeping it simple. "The officers only left an hour ago. It doesn't feel real."

I sat down on a chaise, and Alice laid her head in my lap. I still hadn't seen her face, just a tangle of brown hair.

"Is there anything I can help with?" I asked. "I want to make things as easy on all of you as I can. That's why I'm here."

Lady Ashton sat next to me and ran a hand through Alice's hair. "That is very kind, Rose. Especially considering everything that has happened."

I tapped my fingers across her knuckles for just a moment and offered her a sad smile. "We are family. Always."

She sighed as though the idea was overwhelming, and I suspected she was thinking of her own family. Of how irrevocably it had been changed in the last weeks.

"There isn't much to be done right now. They will send

for us when it comes time to claim Edward's body. In the meantime, the funeral is being arranged and will probably be early next week."

I nodded. Lord Ashton and Catherine were still immobile, and the room was so quiet that even the smallest whisper felt too loud.

I spoke as softly as I could, moving my lips dramatically to better help Lady Ashton follow along with what I was saying. "Now, I'm sorry to ask at such a time, but the letter I received made no mention of a cause of death. Were you told what happened?"

I wanted to tell Lady Ashton that I'd seen Edward only that morning and he had been in perfect health. However, I did not want to have to explain why I was there, so I kept it to myself.

Lady Ashton sighed, and then sobbed once, her fingers folded over her lips. She took a shaky breath and set her shoulders. She closed her eyes as she spoke.

"It was a fight amongst some of the inmates as he was being transported back to his cell," she said, thinly veiled emotion breaking through occasionally in the form of a sudden pitch change. "A fellow prisoner murdered him with a makeshift weapon. As far as we know, there was no cause."

My vision went black along the edges. I tried to inhale, but my lungs felt arid and stiff. Edward was murdered as he was being transported back to his cell? Back to his cell from where? I wanted to ask, but deep down I already knew. Edward had been killed as he was led away from our visit this morning. Moments after I'd nodded to him through the metal doorway, promising to return another day, he had been murdered. I closed my eyes and took a deep breath.

There was a hand on my shoulder. "You have a kind

heart, Rose," Lady Ashton said. "I know Edward did not treat you...well."

That was an understatement, but I also knew how difficult it was for Lady Ashton to admit in that moment, and I was grateful to her for seeing and respecting my unique position. However, she had also deeply misunderstood the cause of my distress. It was not that Edward had died, though that was sad. Rather, the idea that he had died only moments after I'd last seen him—perhaps, even before I had left the prison grounds—made me feel sick to my stomach.

"Regardless of everything, Edward's passing is a tragedy. Incomprehensible. I only wish to ease your burden in any way I can."

Lady Ashton pursed her lips together, fresh tears welling in her swollen eyes, and then laid her head on my shoulder. We stayed that way for a long time, Alice in my lap, Lady Ashton on my shoulder, until the sun burned low in the sky, leaking through the drawn shades in ribbons of gold, reminding us all that though we were mourning, time continued on.

3

W hile in the sitting room, surrounded by Edward's grieving family and the soft sound of their sobs, I came to a realization: the Chess Master had murdered Edward.

I couldn't know for sure, of course, but it seemed like the only answer that made sense. I'd gone to Edward to discover the Chess Master's identity, and just as he'd promised to tell me everything he knew, he was murdered. Who else would have had a motive? True, I didn't understand the inner workings of a prison. Edward could have been in a feud with a fellow inmate over a lunch table or a stolen cigarette. But it seemed much more likely to me that the Chess Master had silenced Edward before he could spill any secrets.

It was a disturbing thought—the long reach of the Chess Master. I knew it was unlikely that he had physically walked into the prison and murdered Edward. And besides, we knew another inmate had done the deed. So, I had to assume the Chess Master had a connection inside the prison who he had called upon to help him. How many other connections did he have throughout the city? Edward had told me the man was powerful, but I hadn't appreciated the weight of that until now.

Edward's murder was upsetting, and my heart broke for his family, but I also had to admit that much of my sadness stemmed from losing a possible connection to the Chess Master. Edward was the only person I knew who had seen the man face to face. I'd rested all of my hopes on Edward leading me to my enemy, and now he was gone.

I tried to be there for the Beckingham family, fetching servants for them when they needed food or water, piling blankets over their shoulders when they were cold, peeling them off when they became hot. Lord Ashton eventually moved from his place at the window and took up a perch on the edge of a wooden chair in the corner. He looked uncomfortable, but I suspected that was the point. My uncle was punishing himself. For what exactly, I didn't know, but somehow, he felt responsible for Edward's death.

Catherine left the sitting room before dinner the first day and retired to her room. She scarcely came out again and wouldn't open the door when anyone knocked. Unlike everyone else, she hadn't allowed herself to cry. And to be fair, I could understand her lack of emotion. Just weeks prior, her brother had murdered her secret lover, Mr. Matcham, and now her brother had been murdered. It was a confusing turn of events.

Alice and Lady Ashton took the traditional path of mourning. They alternated between moments of tears and laughter, remembering something fond about Edward with a smile, and then descending into a fit of sobs. They grew restless in the sitting room, and then would nearly collapse with fatigue on a walk around the perimeter of the house. It was just as well because newspaper reporters hearing the news of Edward's passing began to descend upon the home.

The servants turned them away and, when a few persistent journalists refused to go away, I threatened to alert the authorities.

"*Miss Beckingham, how does it feel now that your attempted murderer is dead?*"

"*Do you believe the murder was random or a planned attack?*"

"*When will the funeral be held and who will claim the body?*"

They were vultures, circling around the family's grief, eager for any scrap of news. I tried to keep the family away from the brunt of it, but they heard the questions float from the doorway into the house, they knew their family had become a spectacle. It was for that reason exactly that, on the third day, Lady Ashton pulled me aside.

"I cannot allow my girls to stay here any longer," she said, shaking her head. The first day I'd seen my aunt, her eyes had been swollen with tears. Now, they looked dry and sunken, as though she had cried out all the moisture in her body. Blue circled under her eyes in deep pools, displaying her lack of sleep.

"I would offer to let you stay at my home, but Aseem has sent word that it isn't much better there," I admitted. The boy had written that morning that he and George had spent the past few days dispersing reporters from in front of the house.

"It won't be better anywhere in London," Lady Ashton said, bordering on anger.

"Things will calm down eventually. There will be another news story and you all will be forgotten."

Lady Ashton jerked slightly at my words and I realized the potential cruelty in them. The idea that her son could be so easily forgotten was certainly not a nice one. However, I decided not to dwell on it.

"My girls will never have a normal life here," she said, shaking her head. "Not the life their father and I imagined for them. They will always be associated with this story, with a scandal they had nothing to do with. It isn't fair."

I thought of the scandal that had turned my own life upside down—the double axe murder of my parents. Even if I hadn't been so young at the time of their deaths, I would have fled New York City. My life was going to be defined by that trauma. To everyone I had known, I would be the girl with the murdered parents, whose brother had disappeared afterward and later been accused of the crime. My life would no longer be my own. Luckily, I'd been taken in as an orphan and eventually sent to India, before ultimately ending up in England.

"I'm sorry, aunt," I said, pulling her towards the dining room table and helping her sit down. "I'm sure everything will be all right in the end."

I didn't know this to be true—no one could—but I hoped it for them. Lady Ashton nodded and then, suddenly, looked up at me, eyes blazing.

"You said you came here to ease our burden, Rose. Is that true?" she asked.

I nodded. "Yes, of course. Anything you need."

She clasped my hands in her own, her fingers trembling against my skin. "You have been around the world, Rose. You have experienced other cultures, travelled aboard large ships. You are much more worldly than my girls."

My brow furrowed, trying to uncover the meaning behind my aunt's words. "What are you saying?"

"Would you travel with them?" she asked. "I have a sister in New York, the girls' aunt. She could take them in while their father and I deal with things here."

I released a long breath, trying to think. I had spent so

much time focused on getting to London, it would be strange now to return to the city I'd once called home.

"I'm not sure the girls will agree," I said.

"Alice will love it, and Catherine will go if I tell her I need her to watch her sister." Lady Ashton responded quickly enough that I knew she'd already thought about all of this. "There will be further investigation into the murder Edward committed, and then an investigation into Edward's own death. This story will be in the papers for the better part of a year. I have to do what I can to protect the girls from public speculation and cruelty and sending them away is the best I can do."

She was right, it would be a big story. A well-known family's fall from grace would keep Londoners eagerly reading for months. Going to New York was a good idea for the girls, but I wasn't sure it was a good idea for me. I felt tantalizingly close to discovering the identity of the Chess Master, and I had to assume I'd lose any chance of uncovering the truth when I was half a world away. Not to mention, Achilles Prideaux was still looking into the case of my missing brother Jimmy. He hadn't discovered anything yet, but the investigation would take a back seat if we lost contact. Going away could derail everything I'd done to try and find Jimmy.

However, perhaps going back to New York City, being in the place where the murders of my parents had occurred a decade ago, would lead to fresh discoveries. I could talk to the police there and see if anyone had reopened the case. Plus, New York had been the last place Jimmy was seen. I'd looked for him before being taken to the orphanage, but I was no longer a child now. Perhaps, I'd be able to pick up his trail this time.

"I know I'm asking a lot of you, Rose," Lady Ashton said,

biting her lower lip. It looked broken and bruised from the nervous habit. "And do not feel as though you have to agree. It is just that you are one of the only people I would entrust my girls with."

"I'll do it." The words were out of my mouth before I could second guess them. Lady Ashton's eyes widened in shock and then a smile pulled up the edges of her mouth. "Dear, sweet Rose. I can truly never repay you for this kindness."

"You do not need to repay me anything," I said. "You took me in after I was orphaned. You gave me a home until I could find my way in a new city. You gave me a family when mine had been stolen from me. Truly, it is I who must repay you."

Lady Ashton's lip trembled and then her arms were around me, her round head pressed into the space between my chin and shoulder.

"You are too good, Rose. Far too good."

I patted my aunt's back and wondered how she would feel if she knew I wasn't Rose at all. If she knew that, had I never lied about my identity, I wouldn't have been at the family estate to see that Edward was arrested as a murderer, meaning he wouldn't have been in prison, and he wouldn't have been murdered by a fellow prisoner.

Not only was I paying Lady Ashton back for the kindness she had shown me, but for the immeasurable heartache I had caused her. My lies had done more damage than I ever intended, and perhaps leaving London was one way I could set things right.

4

In the days that followed, preparations for the journey to New York began. Lady Ashton sent a letter to her sister immediately, asking if she could house myself, Catherine, and Alice. My aunt didn't have a clear idea of how long she wanted to send the girls away, so the letter simply said "indefinitely," which meant I had a great deal of packing to do.

Aseem was against the idea, though he wouldn't say so outright. He simply expressed his displeasure by packing remarkably slowly and making subtle remarks about things I'd miss about the city and the length of the journey.

"Monsieur Prideaux has become a dear friend, has he not? Won't you miss him?"

"New York City is crowded. I've never been, but you hear stories."

"You really intend to board another ship after what happened on the last one?"

Finally, after days of this, I pulled him aside.

"Aseem, you do realize you will still have a job in my household when I leave?"

He looked at me, eyes blank. So, I continued.

"For the entire time I am away in New York, you will live here in this house and manage it for me. You will carry on as though nothing has changed, and I will be sure you are paid as usual."

"I will," he said, the two words somewhere between a statement and a question.

I nodded. "Yes, of course. I wouldn't dream of leaving you without employment or housing. You have been too loyal for that kind of treatment."

Aseem smiled, and suddenly, his packing speed increased ten-fold. He became so efficient I was almost offended. Did he want me out of the house? Was he looking forward to it?

Expecting her sister to reply that she would be charmed to accept us into her home as guests, Lady Ashton booked us all passage aboard a ship set to sail at the end of the week. It hardly seemed possible that I could be leaving London after such a short time spent there. It had only been a few months. Yet, I also found myself excited by the adventure and the possibility to return to the city where I was born, where I'd last seen my brother.

On the morning I received the letter from Lady Ashton outlining mine and the girls' travel plans, I decided to take a break from packing up the house and go for a walk. It had been so long since I'd been in New York that I could hardly remember the weather, but I couldn't imagine it could ever be as beautiful as in London. My early morning walks had become a cherished daily ritual. Whether the sky was blue or an overcast gray, the city seemed to sing. Everything took on a shimmery quality, like I'd stepped into an oil painting. I passed people on the street and imagined I knew the inner workings of their minds, that they were all actors in a play and I was the only spectator. The walk gave me a sense of calm that almost nothing else could. And on this morning, on what I expected to be one of my last London walks for a while, I found myself outside the iron gates of the cemetery where Rose's parents had been buried.

I'd visited the cemetery the day after I arrived in the city, wanting to pay my respects to the people who had been my employers and the parents of my dearest friend in the world. Now, I went again to thank them for my current financial stability—having inherited their fortune—and because I felt Rose would want me to. If Rose were truly alive, she would certainly visit her parents' grave often—or, at least, the grave marker that honored their memories, their bodies being too ruined to send home for a proper burial. However, I had not visited them nearly as often as I should have, and I wanted to try and make amends before I left the city.

A thick canopy of leaves hung over the headstones, dripping morning dew onto the mossy ground below. The cemetery was well-maintained and beautifully landscaped, stones pressed into the grass forming a path, the dappled sunlight peeking through the trees. I followed the route through the center of the cemetery for a while until a narrowed path branched off to the right. At the end of that path were the Beckinghams. Arranging the fabric of my navy taffeta dress around my legs so it wouldn't sink into the soft earth beneath me, I dropped down to my knees in front of the gravestone and folded my hands in my lap.

Unlike the first time I'd visited the Beckinghams, I didn't have much to say. It simply felt nice to sit there with them, remembering the people they had been. I thought of Rose— her tinkling laugh and bright white smile. She had been my only friend for so long, and I still felt lost without her. Thankfully, the weeks and months since her death had been busy and full, meaning I had little time to think about the loss. But sitting there in the quiet of the cemetery, the gravity of it all fell upon me. Silent tears slipped down my cheeks.

"Mademoiselle Rose?"

My entire body flinched, and I jumped to my feet. As soon as I saw the tall, lean man standing in front of me, I realized I should have recognized the French accent immediately.

"I'm sorry to have frightened you," Achilles Prideaux said, shifting his cane from one hand to the other and planting it firmly back on the ground. I knew from our time aboard the RMS Star of India together that a secret blade was concealed inside the end of his cane and could be released with a flick of his wrist.

"I just wasn't expecting anyone," I said, dabbing at my eyes. "I didn't even hear you approach."

"I was on the street when I saw you turn into the cemetery," he said. "I had plans to visit you later this afternoon, but when I saw you here, I thought now would be as good a time as any. Was I wrong? Should I call upon you this afternoon instead?"

"No, no, of course not," I said, holding out a hand to Monsieur Prideaux. "Now is the perfect time. I actually wanted to speak to you, as well, so this is a lovely surprise."

Achilles turned partially away from me, one elbow extended, and then used his other hand to grab my hand and wrap it around his forearm. I couldn't tell if I was imagining things or not, but it seemed as if his fingers lingered on mine for a moment longer than necessary. And I would have sworn I felt the slightest brush of his thumb across my knuckle.

"What did you wish to speak with me about?" Achilles asked as we followed the narrow stone path back towards the central walkway that led to the gates.

"After you, Monsieur Prideaux," I said. I couldn't pin down exactly why, but I felt nervous about breaking the news.

"Feeling generous today?" he asked, eyebrow quirked. He gave me a playful smile and then in the next second, his face had taken on a somber expression. "I actually came to talk to you about the man you hired me to investigate, Jimmy Dennet."

It had been so long since I'd heard anyone say his name that I felt exposed, as if Achilles had peeled back my skin. I swallowed. "Yes?"

"I've turned up some troubling information that I thought you should be made aware of. You said he was an old acquaintance, so I do not know your relationship exactly, but Jimmy Dennet was accused of a very disturbing crime back in New York."

"Was he?" I asked, trying to sound surprised, but it rang false even to my ears.

"I do not wish to distress you, Mademoiselle Rose, but he was charged with a double axe murder."

I gasped and Achilles continued as though I hadn't made a sound. "He disappeared after the crimes and hasn't been seen since. I would highly advise you not to seek out such a dangerous man. I know my advice hasn't been worth much to you in the past, but I implore you to listen to me now. Jimmy Dennet is not good company to keep."

"Thank you, Monsieur Prideaux," I said, keeping my hand on his arm, but pulling away from him slightly. "I appreciate you looking into this for me. Send a bill for your trouble and I will have Aseem take care of the payment."

Achilles stopped moving and grabbed my hand, bending his head to look into my eyes. "I do not care about the money, Rose. I need to know that you will not go looking for this man any longer. I need to know you aren't going to find yourself in yet another dangerous situation."

I smiled, but it felt strained and awkward. "Don't worry about me. I can take care of myself. I just appreciate you helping me out."

Achilles let go of my hand and stepped away. "What is your relationship with Jimmy Dennet, may I ask?"

"Friends," I said. "Old friends. I haven't seen him in ten years."

"Well, your *friend* doesn't seem to be so friendly, and I would caution you to stay away from him," Achilles repeated.

He widened his eyes knowingly as he spoke, and I knew he could tell I was lying. It had been foolish to hire a world-famous detective to look into Jimmy's whereabouts for me. I was lucky he hadn't discovered my true identity yet. Plus, I was putting Jimmy at risk. If Achilles did find him, there was a good chance he would alert the police to Jimmy's location, and my brother would be arrested whether he truly was guilty or not.

Going to New York suddenly seemed like a good idea. It would put some distance between Monsieur Prideaux and myself, and hopefully he would move on to other cases and forget about me entirely.

"Actually, soon you won't need to worry about me anymore," I said, folding my hands behind my back and walking ahead of him on the path.

"What do you mean?" Achilles asked.

"I'm leaving London," I said, turning to face him. "I'm going with my cousins to their aunt's house in New York City. I assume you heard what befell Edward."

His jaw tightened, and he nodded tersely. "I heard the news. Forgive me, I should have offered my condolences sooner."

"It's quite all right. We both know I was not exceedingly close to Edward. The point is that the news has been hard on my family, and Lady Ashton asked me to escort her daughters to New York."

"For how long?"

"Indefinitely," I shrugged. "I think it will be a good thing for me. I've found nothing but trouble in this city. Perhaps, it's time for a fresh start."

Prideaux's top lip twitched and his eyes shifted nervously. "You will have to give me your new address, so I know where to send any other discoveries about Jimmy. And the Chess Master, of course. I'm still looking into that for you."

My stomach twisted. "Actually, I won't be requiring your services any longer."

He stepped back, looking at me as though I'd slapped him.

"I appreciate everything you've done," I said. "You have been a friend to me in my time in London and I'm grateful. Between Edward's death and the move, I have simply lost interest in the matters I asked you to pursue."

"I see," Monsieur Prideaux said, crossing his hands on top of his cane, one eyebrow arched suspiciously. "Then, I suppose this is goodbye."

"I suppose so," I said, surprised at how abruptly our quasi-friendship was ending.

"I hope New York is all you expect it to be," Achilles said. "Good day, Mademoiselle Rose."

With that, the Frenchman turned on his heel and disappeared down the street.

5

L ater that afternoon, Aseem and I were back to packing with vigor. Parts of the house that would not be used in my absence were deep cleaned and we would drop cloths over all of the furniture to ward away dust. It still felt surreal that I would be leaving so shortly after buying my own London home.

As I had suspected, Catherine didn't want to go to New York, but when Lady Ashton told her she needed to accompany her younger sister, Catherine's own sense of self-importance persuaded her. She liked feeling important, and Lady Ashton preyed on that. Alice didn't need any persuading. She had already put together a list of all the famous places in the city she was going to take me. I wished I could tell her I had already seen most of them as a little girl.

My conversation with Achilles Prideaux weighed heavily on my mind most of the day. I knew he'd suspected I was lying about several things and I couldn't shake the feeling that he would uncover my secret. What would he do if he did discover the truth? Would he be angry with me for lying to him? Would he tell Lord and Lady Ashton? Would they take back Rose's inheritance, or what I had obtained of it so far, through my monthly allowance, and leave me alone and destitute on the streets of New York? The idea terrified me, but there was also a sense of cosmic justice to the idea. Being back on the streets would mean my life would have come completely full circle.

A knock at the door pulled me from my thoughts and I dropped the dusting cloth on the table as I moved towards the entrance hall. Aseem whipped past the dining room to answer it, but I stopped him.

"I'll get it, Aseem. Thank you," I said.

"Are you sure, Miss Rose?"

I nodded, and he disappeared back into the kitchen. The last time he'd answered the door, I'd learned of Edward's murder. Perhaps, I was being superstitious, but I thought it would be best if I answered it myself. Plus, somewhere in the back of my mind, I thought I would see Monsieur Prideaux standing on the porch. Of course, I knew we didn't have anything else to say to one another, but I had hoped to part as friends, and I didn't like the way we had left things at the cemetery.

When I opened the door, however, I was met with an unfamiliar figure. At my doorstep was a short, round man with a thick gray mustache that stretched wider than his face, and a brown hat atop his head.

"Good afternoon. Are you Miss Rose Beckingham?" the man asked, his words quick and clipped.

"Yes, I am. And you are?"

"Henry Branwell, Miss. Might I come inside and speak to you about a rather sensitive matter?" the man asked, gesturing past me into the house.

I pulled the door closed behind me and stepped onto the porch, put off by his brazen attitude. "I'm sorry, but I'd rather speak with you outside."

He nodded, his smile faltering as he turned to see several groups of people walking down the sidewalk. He lowered his voice as he continued. "Of course. That is no problem. I received your information from a Mister Charles Barry. I hope you don't mind me bothering you unannounced. I would have written, but I didn't want the letter to be intercepted."

It took me a second to recognize the name of Barry. I'd only met the man once. Charles Barry and his sister Vivian were guests of the Beckinghams at their country estate. They were glued to each other's sides and solely interested in Catherine and Edward, respectively. I wouldn't have remembered the name at all except the weekend we met happened to be the very same weekend that Edward killed Mr. Matcham and tried to kill me. No matter how much I wished otherwise, the details of that weekend were burned into my memory.

"Why did you need my information?" I asked, confused about why Charles Barry would be mentioning my name to anyone, let alone a stranger. I was also confused as to why this man seemed to think he was on a secret and urgent mission.

"I have a very private matter to discuss with you involving a stolen painting," the man said, voice so low I had to lean in to hear him.

I stared at him, still not understanding, and I could tell Henry Branwell was beginning to doubt whether he was at the right house or not. Honestly, so was I.

He said, "Charles described you as a capable investigator."

I was shaking my head before Henry even finished the sentence. "No, I'm sorry. There must be some confusion. I'm not—"

"He said he witnessed you successfully investigating a murder," Henry interrupted, his voice rising higher in pitch, nearing a controlled hysteria. "He claimed an art theft would be no trouble for you."

Charles hadn't witnessed me solving anything. I had investigated privately and didn't talk to Charles much at all the entire weekend we were in Somerset. But I had been the person to capture Edward, and perhaps he had been more impressed by that than I'd realized. He, of course, couldn't know that I'd only stumbled upon the truth by accident. My investigation had pointed towards Lady Ashton as the culprit, and only when I saw Edward burying the vial he'd used to poison poor Mr. Matcham did I put the pieces of the puzzle together. Part of me was flattered by Charles' recommendation, but I also didn't know how I felt about him giving my name away to strange men with even stranger sounding crimes.

"That is very kind of Mr. Barry, but I assure you, a real detective would be much more apt to take on this case. Have you spoken to the police?"

Mr. Branwell waved a hand to stop me. "I chose to speak with you because this theft is a rather delicate matter. If it can be managed, we would like to handle this matter privately and avoid calling the police. The board of directors doesn't want this information to spread much further than our tight circle."

"Board of directors?" I asked. I knew indulging the man was irresponsible, considering: one, he seemed to be nearing a mental breakdown, and two, I had no intention of taking his case since I would soon be leaving the country. But still, my curiosity won out.

The man nodded. "I work for a major museum in London. You will have to forgive me for being vague. I cannot give away any more information than necessary. As I already said, no one wants news of this crime leaking to the press. That is the last thing we need. What Oscar Wilde said about there being nothing worse than not being talked about is wrong. We don't want anyone talking about this."

"I understand," I said, growing weary of his repeated insistence upon secrecy.

"But," Mr. Branwell said, leaning towards me, eyes darting wildly from left to right, "I'm here because a valuable painting— "The Chess Match" —has been stolen, and we are hoping to catch the culprit and bring about it's safe return."

"The painting was called 'The Chess Match?'" I asked.

He nodded. "It featured a man and a woman enthralled in a game of chess. It was painted by a very distinguished English painter who only died a few years ago. 'The Chess Match' was one of his final works before holding the brush became too difficult for him. It is worth a great deal. We were lucky to have it in our collection, and I hate to think what will happen to it without the proper care."

Henry continued talking about how necessary it was to properly care for fine art, regulating the temperature and access to direct sunlight, but my mind was spinning off in another direction. Could the name of the painting be a message to me from the Chess Master? Or, was it merely a coincidence? Lately, I'd stopped believing in coincidences. A painting of a man and woman playing a game of chess had gone missing and, out of all the detectives, both public and private, in London, the museum somehow came across my name. Everything seemed designed for a purpose; I only had to figure out what that purpose was.

On the other hand, even if the theft was carried out with the express purpose of me becoming involved, I had to ask whether I wanted to be involved. The Chess Master had brought me nothing but trouble, and I had good reason to believe he had killed Edward. What would stop him from doing the same to me? Still, the mystery was intriguing.

Henry was still carrying on when I interrupted him with a small cough. He stopped, wide-eyed as though he'd just awoken from a dream, and folded his hands behind his back.

"After seeing your passion for the museum and this particular piece of artwork, I can't deny my services," I said. Henry clapped his hands together, his mustache twitching with a smile, but I continued over his cheers. "I am already scheduled to leave the country soon, so I cannot promise that I will see this investigation through from start to finish, but I will do what I can to see that the culprit is found. Or, at the very least, that the investigation begins on the right foot."

"That is marvelous, Miss Beckingham. Absolutely brilliant. On behalf of the entire Board of Directors, I'd like to offer our sincerest thanks."

He reached for my hand to kiss it, but I politely pulled it away, tucking it behind my back. "I haven't solved the case yet, so you ought to hold your gratitude until then."

Henry stood straight and pulled his face into as neutral an expression as he could manage, but it was clear he had been set upon procuring me, and it was difficult for him to contain his delight upon having accomplished his aim.

"Shall I take you to the museum now?" he asked, turning sideways and gesturing to the sidewalk.

"I suppose there is no time like the present." I pulled the door closed behind me and set off into the city with Henry Branwell waddling along beside me.

6

The museum was housed in a building designed to resemble a Roman temple. A large stone pediment with a relief sculpture of men charging into ancient battle sat atop fluted columns as thick as one-hundred-year-old tree trunks. Inside, the columns continued, spanning the entire space from front to back in two even rows, taking on the brunt of weight from the stone roof. Skylights carved into the roof cast rectangles of daylight that moved with the sun across the floor. Windows also dotted the walls, giving the cavernous space a surprising warmth. Individual exhibition spaces were carved out with thin, movable walls.

"It's beautiful," I said, neck craned back so I could stare up at the ceiling and the patch of blue sky beyond it.

Having already secured my help, Henry Branwell seemed uninterested in indulging me in idle chitchat. He hummed at my adoration for the building, but kept moving, his legs carrying him directly to the back corner of the room, through a door, and into a long hallway without a single window. Our footsteps tapped against the tile floor, echoing off the stone walls, before we stopped in front of a wooden door with Henry's name carved in gold letters next to it. He opened the door and ushered me inside.

His office was a museum in itself. The bones of what appeared to be a bat were pinned to a sheet of cloth and draped across a shelf on the wall, a pile of river stones was unexplainedly arranged next to that, and taking up a shelf entirely to themselves, were a smattering of empty shadow-boxes, some with broken glass panes. Henry's desk was covered in precarious piles of papers and he had three different cups full of pens and pencils.

Distracted by the oddities littering the small room, I almost didn't notice the mousy man sitting in the corner, his arms folded across his chest as though he were afraid to take up too much space. He smiled as I looked at him but said nothing. I couldn't even be sure he was breathing. Though, I couldn't blame him. I found myself taking shallower breaths, as well, afraid a strong exhale would topple the papers on the desk.

"Miss Beckingham," Mr. Branwell said, strolling into the room and dropping into the leather chair behind the desk. "This is one of our guards, Mr. Tomlin. He is here to give you his testimony of the events of that night."

I wanted to ask how long Mr. Tomlin had been waiting in Henry Branwell's small office and how they had been so certain I would come to the museum to help them investigate, but I decided it didn't matter. I had agreed to come with Mr. Branwell, and it was nice that Mr. Tomlin was already there to catch me up on what happened. Once I was seated in the tufted chair opposite Mr. Tomlin, I crossed my ankles and gestured for him to begin.

"I was in the main room the night of the theft," he said, his voice just as high-pitched as I would have guessed, based on his small size. "When I made my rounds at eleven P.M., the painting was hanging on the wall where it usually is, but when I passed back by at one A.M., the space on the wall was empty and the back door was left open."

"Does the museum have an alarm system?" I asked.

Mr. Tomlin nodded.

"But it didn't go off?" I asked.

Mr. Tomlin shook his head.

I sighed. Clearly, I'd need to draw the answers out of Mr. Tomlin one inane question at a time.

"Do you have any idea why it wouldn't have gone off?" I asked.

His lips pursed, and he shrugged. "Maybe the thief knew the code."

"That's preposterous," Mr. Branwell said. "All of our employees are thoroughly vetted before being hired. No one with any kind of criminal past is allowed to work in the museum. I trust our employees wholeheartedly."

"Do you have another explanation?" I asked.

Mr. Branwell's cheeks reddened as he thought. "It could be a malfunction with the equipment or the door hadn't been shut properly before the alarm system was turned on."

"Would you have noticed if the door was open at ii P.M., Mr. Tomlin?" I asked.

The man nodded. "I would have, yes."

I turned back to Mr. Branwell. "And have you had any issues with the equipment in the past or would this have been the first time it malfunctioned?"

"It would be the first time," Mr. Branwell said, his mustache bristling.

"Then, I believe we would be wise to start our investigation inside the museum," I announced. "It is more likely that the thief knew the code to the alarm than to think a thief happened to rob the museum on the one night the alarm system decided not to work. And if the thief knew the code to the alarm, it leads me to believe they are either an employee of the museum, or closely connected with an employee."

"My gut tells me it was Peter Grove," Mr. Tomlin said, eyes wide, finger pointed to the ceiling. "He was acting very suspicious that night and I haven't seen him since."

"It has only been two days since we've seen him," Mr. Branwell snapped, eyes narrowed at Mr. Tomlin. "And he asked for time off. I'm sure he will be back as soon as his time is up."

"Peter Grove was working with you the night of the robbery?" I asked Tomlin.

"Well, the shift before mine, Miss. We met up at the start of my shift to exchange keys and check the doors together," he said.

"So, Peter locked the doors that night?"

"We both did," he said.

"Did you both lock each door or did you both separately lock different doors?" I asked.

Mr. Tomlin looked at me, forehead wrinkled in confusion. I looked to Mr. Branwell for help explaining my meaning, but he looked perplexed, as well.

"Explain to me the process of locking the doors," I said with a sigh.

Mr. Tomlin nodded. "It was a ritual we had to make sure two sets of eyes saw to it that every door was properly locked after the museum was closed for the night. It was to make sure neither of us made a mistake and left the place unlocked. You don't want to be the fellow who leaves a museum full of precious art and artifacts exposed for thieves. Though, in this case, it looks as though I might still be that fellow. But anyway, as soon as that was done, I let Peter out the back door, locked it behind him, and went to the security desk."

"Where is the security desk?" I asked.

"Near the back door, tucked away in the corner so as not to be an eyesore," Mr. Tomlin said, as though he was repeating something he'd heard from someone else.

"How much of the museum can you see from the desk?"

"I can show you," Mr. Tomlin said, standing up for the first time. "It's easier than trying to explain it."

I liked the sound of that idea. Mr. Tomlin didn't have much of an instinct for the kinds of questions a detective might ask while investigating a robbery, so asking him so many obvious questions had quickly grown tiresome.

"I do not want the guests to suspect anything is wrong," Mr. Branwell said, his palms flat on his desk.

It was funny. On my doorstep, Mr. Branwell had been all too anxious for me to take the case, but now that I was standing in front of him, ready to get to work, he seemed hesitant. It had all started as soon as I'd mentioned the possibility of someone inside the museum being the culprit. As much as I doubted Mr. Branwell was the suspect, I couldn't rule out the possibility.

"I am nothing if not discreet, sir," I said.

He sighed and led Mr. Tomlin and me from the room and back down the hallway towards the main gallery space. In the short time we'd been in the room, the gallery had filled significantly.

"There is always a late afternoon rush," Mr. Branwell said, walking in a determined, straight line from the hallway to the opposite wall.

The crowd seemed to be mostly school children and young couples, most likely stopping in before a night out in the city. For a brief moment, I thought how nice it would be to lead such an ordinary life. It had never been possible for me. In India, there had hardly been time or opportunity for me to meet a man. And now, my life had become such a tangled web of lies, not to mention murder after murder, that finding anyone seemed impossible.

"Are you coming, Miss Beckingham?"

I turned to see Mr. Tomlin waiting for me and gave him a warm smile. He seemed like a nice man, and I hoped he wouldn't turn out to be the thief. I had been made a fool by enough criminals, I'd hate for it to happen again. Mr. Branwell hadn't stopped to wait for me and was already across the room, standing in front of a noticeably empty wall.

As I approached, I noticed a small sign. *This piece has been removed for restoration.*

"I assume this is where the stolen painting hung?" I asked quietly.

"Yes, but there is no need to announce such a thing," Mr. Branwell hissed, glaring daggers at me. He shook his head, as though dispelling a thought, and took a deep breath. "From this vantage point, the very corner of the security desk is just beyond that corner," he said, pointing to the far corner of the museum.

I followed his finger but didn't see the desk at all, so I began moving in the direction he had pointed. It wasn't until I'd crossed the entire space and turned the corner that I could see the desk. It would have been impossible for anyone sitting at the security desk to see the wall where "The Chess Match" had been hanging the night it was stolen.

When Mr. Branwell and Mr. Tomlin caught up to me, I asked the guard how much time he spent at the desk during his shift.

"I don't keep records of it," he said.

"Just a guess is fine," I said. "A percentage. Half? Less than half? More than half?"

He twisted his lips up in thought, his eyes cast towards the ceiling. "More than half. Maybe, seventy-five percent?"

I nodded and turned to Mr. Branwell. "Do you have the home address for Peter Grove?"

"I have the address for all the employees, but what do you need with that?"

"You asked me to investigate, and that is what I intend to do. At this moment, Peter Grove is my only suspect. I would like to rule him out, if possible."

"It's a waste of time," Mr. Branwell said. "I would not hire a thief."

"No one knowingly hires a thief, Mr. Branwell. And it would be no shame on you if you had. Even the wisest among us can be fooled," I said, though I didn't believe Mr. Branwell was anywhere near the wisest person I'd met.

Reluctantly, and very much against his better judgment, Mr. Branwell walked me back to his office, dug through his folder of employee files, and retrieved Peter Grove's information.

"Promise me you will not trouble him," he said.

"Me? Trouble?" I asked, a mischievous smile on my lips. "Never."

Mr. Branwell looked less than convinced as Mr. Tomlin and I stepped out of his office and into the hallway. We were nearly to the door that led back into the museum when Mr. Tomlin stopped and turned to me, eyes serious.

"I know what Mr. Branwell said, but Peter Grove has always looked like trouble to me. We didn't start locking the doors together until he was hired. I didn't trust him. In his first week on the job, he was so forgetful. Always leaving the doors unlocked, forgetting to set the alarm, taking his breaks out of turn." Mr. Tomlin looked down the hallway towards Mr. Branwell's door to be sure he hadn't emerged, and then began talking again, his voice lower than before. "There is a rumor going around that Peter Grove is Mr. Branwell's nephew on his wife's side. I'm not saying Mr. Branwell isn't being impartial, but..."

"But he might have a soft spot in his heart for his nephew?" I finished.

Mr. Tomlin nodded. "I just think you should look into him fully as a suspect, no matter what Mr. Branwell says. I'm nervous that I will catch all the blame if the true culprit can't be caught."

I reached out and placed a hand on Mr. Tomlin's thin shoulder. "Don't worry. I will do my best to ensure the guilty parties are caught and brought to justice, whoever they may be."

That thought didn't rally Mr. Tomlin as much as I'd hoped it would, and he still looked scattered and nervous as we parted ways and he walked back over to the security desk in the corner. I walked straight through the front doors and out onto the sidewalk. Destination: Peter Grove's flat.

7

Navigating the center of London was like walking through a minefield. One block could be lovely, filled with families out for afternoon strolls and men and women who would nod politely to every person they passed. And then the next block over was soot-covered shacks and people you'd be afraid to meet in a dark alley. Peter Grove, unfortunately, lived in the latter.

I checked the address Mr. Branwell had given me three times before I felt confident I'd found the right place. His building was a tall brick structure with a dark-colored roof that sat on top like a cap. It looked like it had once been nice, but time had not been kind to the building. Rust stains marred the corners where rainwater poured out of overflowing gutters, the cement stairs leading up to the main door were cracked with large weeds growing up through the spaces, and garbage filled the bins along the sidewalks and spilled out into the road. Everything looked and felt gray.

I was still half a block away from Peter's building when the front door opened and a young man with messy black hair stepped out. His suit hung off his shoulders like he was a child playing dress up in his father's clothes, and his shoes were scuffed and worn. I was wondering whether the man might be who I was there to see when a blonde woman two stories above him stuck her head through an open window and whistled down to him.

"If you come home stumbling, you'll be sleeping on the stoop," she said through a haze of smoke, a cigarette pinched between her long, bony fingers. "I mean it, Peter."

The man, who I now knew as Peter, waved a hand at the woman as she ducked back inside the flat. He took off down the street, his shoulders stooped forward, hands deep in his pockets, head lowered against the world. He looked like a man who was up to no good. I followed him but kept a safe distance of half a block between us. There were enough other people on the street that I knew I wouldn't draw any attention.

He walked endlessly, seemingly with no purpose, and I did my best to keep up, but my heels were not as forgiving as Peter's worn in oxfords. We moved from one neighborhood to the next, through business districts and residential. I kept waiting for him to duck into a building or hail a cab, but he just kept walking. He looked around occasionally, but there didn't seem to be any sort of suspicion to the act, merely a look about for the sake of a look about. At some point, I began to wonder whether I hadn't caught him on a simple leisurely stroll. Then, finally, Peter glanced to his left and his right, took a quick peek over his shoulder in my direction, and then satisfied no one was paying him any particular attention, he ducked off into the alley.

My feet were sore and, I suspected, bleeding from the exercise, but I quickened my pace to catch up to Peter before he could slip away. When I reached the alley, I took a tight turn around the corner, hoping to stay close to the brick wall of the building next to it and remain in the shadows, unseen. Instead, I nearly ran smack into a man leaning against the wall, arms crossed over his chest.

The sudden appearance of the figure surprised me, and I yelped, about to apologize when I realized I was standing in front of Peter Grove.

"I thought you were following me," he said, his voice a low growl. "Now that it is confirmed, I'd like to know why."

I'd always prided myself on my ability to talk my way out of tight corners, but Peter Grove had completely and utterly caught me off guard. I had truly believed he hadn't taken any notice of me over the last hour. And, I was a little embarrassed at my own confidence. Clearly, it was unearned.

"I don't know what you mean," I said, side-stepping him, pretending I wanted to get around him.

Peter followed my movement, blocking my path. "You have been walking a half block behind me since I left my house. Why? What do you want?"

I hesitated, not sure whether it would be wise to tell him the truth. If he knew he was a suspect in the crime and he had stolen the painting, would it cause him to destroy it? To leave the city? I was weighing my options carefully when Peter grabbed me by the shoulder and pressed me back against the wall, deeper into the shadows of the alley.

My heart caught in my throat and my muscles seized. The street running beside us, which had seemed safe and bustling in the sunlight only moments before, now struck me as rather secluded. Peter struck my shoulder again, not hard, but enough to rattle me, and the truth burst out of me in a fit of self-preservation.

"I'm investigating a case for the museum," I said in a rush. "The stolen painting. You work there, correct?"

Peter's face screwed up in thought and he stepped away from me, pressing his fists to his sides. "Yeah, I work security. That still doesn't explain why you're following me."

I was relieved to see that he had calmed down so easily. Though, it did make me wonder what he thought my purpose could have been. What could be worse than being suspected of theft?

"I'm trying to narrow down my list of suspects," I said, neglecting to tell him that he was my one and only suspect at the moment.

His eyes narrowed. "Did someone say I had something to do with this?"

I opened my mouth to respond, but he continued talking.

"Because that's ridiculous. Beyond ridiculous. I've never stolen a thing in my life. They probably sent you my way because I'm the newest employee, and the lowest ranking."

"Well, I actually sought you out because no one has seen you since the theft."

"I asked for these days off long before the painting was stolen. It isn't suspicious to not show up to work when you aren't meant to be there, is it? Is it a crime to have a life outside my job?"

"No, but—"

Peter let out a frustrated groan and paced back and forth across the alley like a caged animal. "You are on the wrong track, Miss...whoever you are. There are more powerful people than me who need to be investigated."

"Miss Beckingham," I said, holding my hand out.

Peter looked at my hand, and I could tell he was tempted to shake it, but instead he stopped pacing and crossed his arms. "You already know my name, otherwise I'd tell you."

"I do," I said.

He rolled his eyes and huffed. "Well, you are wasting your time with me."

"Who do you think needs to be investigated?" I asked.

He shook his head. "No way, I won't be the man who talks and loses his job. I need this money. My wife's expecting a baby."

"Congratulations," I said.

He continued as if he didn't hear me. "As soon as I give you a name, folks at the museum will have my head."

"I'll use discretion," I said. "No one will know where the information came from."

Instantly, Peter's eyes darted around the alley as though something was flying above his head that I couldn't see. "People have a way of finding things out."

"Is there one person in particular you are worried about?" I asked, wondering whether he didn't have some experience with the Chess Master.

His jaw stiffened, lips clenched, and he shook his head. "Just know that you won't get anything out of me. You'd do well to head back to the museum and start your investigation over because I haven't done anything wrong."

With that, Peter turned on his heel and disappeared around the corner.

WHEN I FINALLY MADE IT home, it was all I could do not to slip my shoes off by the door and fall to the floor. I knew I could have taken a cab home, but I needed to clear my head. It was dark, and no sooner than the door had closed behind me, Aseem and George were in the doorway, their eyes wide.

"What is it?" I asked.

"Where have you been, Miss?" Aseem asked. "You answered the door and then disappeared."

"We nearly called the police," George added.

If it had only been Aseem who was worried, I wouldn't have been bothered at all. The young boy seemed overly concerned for me. But with George nervous, as well, I realized the strain I'd placed on the house.

"I'm sorry. I suppose I should have told you I was going out," I said.

"Especially with the news of Edward Beckingham beginning to spread," George said. "People are angry he will not have his day in court, and they are beginning to take it out on the Beckinghams."

"How?" I asked, the exhaustion I'd been feeling moments before dissipating. "Has something happened? Is the family all right?"

"They are fine, Miss. But I do worry for how long," George said.

Lady Ashton had been worried about what the papers would do with the information of Edward's death and the trouble it could cause for the family. I wondered whether she would move up the departure date if things became bad enough. Even though I'd just taken on the case at the museum, I was now anxious to see it solved.

I left my clutch on the table next to the door and sighed. "Well, no use worrying about what can't be changed."

"Dinner is ready for you, Miss," Aseem said. "It will likely need re-heating."

I hadn't realized how hungry I was until the mention of food. "That sounds wonderful, Aseem. Thank you."

The boy scurried out of the room and George was close behind him, but I called him back to me.

"I was hoping to ask you to do something rather strange for me, George."

He quirked an eyebrow, but nodded.

"There is a man—Peter Grove—I'd like you to keep track of for me. Just for the next few days. I need to know whether he does anything suspicious or out of the ordinary," I said. "And please, feel free to deny me. I don't want you to do anything you are uncomfortable with."

"That is kind of you, Miss, but I trust you wouldn't t put me in a tight spot. Give me the address, and I'll do it."

I had no intention of speaking to Peter Grove again unless it because absolutely unavoidable, but it felt nice to know I would have eyes on him, at least. If he did anything noteworthy, George would be able to report back to me. Still, I couldn't help but wonder whether Peter hadn't been telling me the truth about looking in the wrong place. Which people "higher up" had he been referring to? Higher up within the museum or in the city? Could he have been talking about the Chess Master?

Part of me was beginning to feel paranoid, thinking everything that happened somehow led back to the Chess Master. However, another part of me felt that it would be naïve to think any different. As time went on, it was becoming more and more clear that the Chess Master had his hands in everything that happened in London. It was also becoming clear that, whether I wanted it or not, the Chess Master had me in his sights.

8

L ady Ashton sent over a letter early the next morning warning me not to come to the house. Reporters had been lurking just outside the gate all day, and it was all she could do to send one of her servants out of the house at the break of dawn to deliver the letter. I penned a hasty reply that I would wait for word from her before stopping by and sent it back with the servant. Then, my day entirely freed up, I left for the museum.

Truly, I was glad for the excuse to stay away from the Beckinghams. Familial duty required that I be there in their time of mourning, and I did want to comfort them in whatever way I could. However, I also didn't know how much longer I would be in the city, and I wanted to spend every minute I could trying to catch the art thief and at the same time, hopefully, the Chess Master.

It was early enough that the museum was mostly empty. No more than fifteen people milled around inside, stopping in front of paintings with their hands folded in front of them, as if they would be unable to resist knocking over the priceless pieces of art otherwise. I meandered through the space, weaving from the hallway into one of the rooms and back out again, getting a feel for the layout. The rooms were arranged by region of the world, and secondarily by style. African masks filled one wall, another display was a table decorated with the finest painted china, and massive portraits of historical figures were framed in intricately carved wooden frames. The collections were so interesting it was almost easy to forget I was there for an assignment. Still, my wandering provided some key insights.

From my minimal research, there appeared to be many different blind spots where security was concerned. It would be easy enough for someone to avoid being seen by a guard, even as the rounds were being made for the evening. That was important because it meant someone wouldn't have had to break in to the museum in the night. They would have only needed to stay inside the museum after closing and avoid detection.

Finally, after making it down the left side of the museum and part of the right, I ended up standing in front of the blank space on the wall where 'The Chess Match' should have hung. Based on the amount of space devoted to the piece, I guessed the painting was quite large. So, the person who stole it would have had to remove it from the wall and carry it outside without making a sound, leaving me to wonder how they would have been able to open doors and even walk onto the street outside without catching anyone's notice.

I was still trying to think through how the painting had been stolen when a woman's voice broke into my thoughts.

"Do you really think it is out for restoration?"

I turned to see a tall, thin woman with cropped brown hair that curled delicately around her temples. She wore a forest green cloche hat and a matching velvet dress. Her black heels were shiny and free of marks.

"I suppose so," I said, though I knew the truth. "Why would the museum lie?"

"Maybe they lost it," she whispered playfully, her red lips pulling up into a smirk. "Or it was stolen."

"You think so?" I asked.

She laughed. "No, probably not. But wouldn't that be exciting? I'd rather a thief steal art than ordinary things. It feels so much more cultured."

"Yes, I'd love for all criminals to be more cultured," I said, half in jest, but also to mock the woman for proposing such an absurd thought.

"I only mean it would make the morning paper more fun to read," she said, green eyes bright. "I do tire of reading about people stealing food and money. It's so dull."

It only took one look at the woman to know she had money and plenty of it. It was incredibly likely that she had never endured hunger or poverty. She didn't know what it was like to boil bones for broth and go to bed hungry the way so many people did. The fact that she could so easily dismiss a person who was stealing to avoid starvation as dull told me everything I needed to know about her character. I had very little intention of getting to know her further.

So, attempting to still be polite, I smiled at her, hovered for a few more seconds near the painting, and then turned away to move on and separate myself from the woman. I stepped into the main corridor and was about to turn into the next exhibit when she appeared at my side.

"I came to the museum early in the morning to be alone, but now I find I am rather bored," she said, once again expressing her dislike of dullness. "Could I possibly enjoy the art with you?"

My lips parted. I wanted to turn her down, but I wasn't entirely sure how to without being rude. Despite my rather instant dislike of her, I had never been good at cruelty, whether it was deserved or not.

She extended her hand. "My name is Sophia Carden."

"Rose Beckingham," I said. Almost immediately, I regretted using my own name. The woman had mentioned only moments before that she read the paper every morning, so certainly she had read of Edward's crimes and his subsequent murder. The name Beckingham would be familiar to her and I'd be left to rehash the gruesome details of the previous few weeks, which I'd much rather forget.

Sophia's eyebrows twitched for a moment, as though she had a flash of recognition, but just as quickly as it arrived, it flittered away. Relief rushed through me.

"I prefer portraits to landscapes," she said, speaking as though she were answering a question I'd asked. Sophia looped her arm through mine and pulled me into the next room. "Not just portraits, I suppose. I like paintings that depict humans."

"Why is that?" I asked, deciding not to fight Sophia's presence. I was hoping to speak to a few more museum employees about the painting, but that would clearly have to wait.

"I can walk outside and see a landscape. The sky paints itself every morning and evening and I have a whole garden of flowers in front of my house. No brush can ever compare to the raw, natural beauty of nature. However, human beings can always be perfected. The artist can straighten crooked lines, tuck away stray hairs, and smooth wrinkles. Paintings show people in their perfected form. They are an improvement on reality."

"Human beings are natural," I said. "Just as much a part of nature as any flower."

"Perhaps we once were, but I feel we've separated ourselves too much. We burn coal and blow smoke and send signals and frequencies through the air and water. We are like alien creatures on this planet, so I much prefer to see humans in painted form than in reality."

"Is that why you are at the museum?" I asked.

She nodded. "I come at least once a week. I like to be near the art. Plus, it's nice to get out of the house."

"Once a week? Doesn't that get dull after a while?" I asked. It was odd to me that a woman so set against being bored would choose to do the same activity every week. I knew little about Sophia Carden, but she didn't seem the type for a routine.

"Art never gets dull. Every time I see a painting, I notice something new about it that changes my perspective entirely. You see, just here," she said, stepping towards an oil painting of a mother and child sitting in a chair. "Last week I noticed that the mother's right hand was high up under the baby's arm, as if she were either in the middle of picking the child up or letting it slip from her grasp. But this week, I noticed her left hand. She wears no ring."

"And how does that change your perspective?" The painting to me looked like a portrait of a mother with an unsettled child. I didn't see how there could be so much meaning within it.

"The woman is likely unwed," Sophia said, tilting her head to the side, her brows drawn together. "Last week, I wondered whether she was a good or a bad mother. Whether she was picking her child up to comfort it or setting it down because she didn't want to bother with the tantrum. But this week, I wonder whether she is raising the child alone. Last week, I judged her. This week, I have sympathy for her."

I tilted my head to the same angle as Sophia's and noted the mother's furrowed brow, the angled set to her eyes, the way she drooped back into the chair. Suddenly, I could feel her exhaustion.

"Do you see it?" Sophia asked, turning towards me.

I nodded. "I think I'm beginning to."

"Isn't it wonderful? How a good painting can make you feel?" she asked with a sigh. "I wish 'The Chess Match' hadn't been removed. I'd love to show you the tension in the player's faces, the unspoken animosity in their posture. You'd think the two figures were in a fight to the death rather than in a game of chess. It is one of my favorite paintings in the museum."

My attention piqued at the mention of the stolen painting. "You know the exact painting that has been taken back to be restored?" I asked.

Sophia laughed. "Now you have to believe me when I say I come here every week. I've memorized the paintings on the walls. I hope I haven't revealed too much about myself by saying that."

I raised my brows. What did she mean "revealed too much?" Too much about what?

"You probably think me some kind of freak now," she said, a hand reaching up to brush back her hair. "Though, I suppose I am. I come to the museum once per week, but I'm also part of an art society."

"An art society?" I asked. "What is that?"

"A collection of like-minded people from around the city," she said. "We hold various charity events throughout the year to raise donations for the museum. It allows the museum to curate art from around the world and grow their collection."

"That sounds fun," I said.

"Oh, it is," Sophia said, turning to grab my arm with both of her hands. "Actually, we are holding a function tonight. It will be dinner and drinks, but mostly conversation. You should come."

I was already shaking my head, though some part of me realized what a good opportunity it would be. I could talk to the art community in the city and see if anyone had any idea where an art thief might be able to sell a famous painting. Because I highly doubted the thief stole the painting simply to hang it on their own wall. No, it was only worth as much as someone would pay for it. And a party full of rich art lovers seemed like an ideal place to start looking for a buyer.

"Please, Rose. I promise I will stay by your side the entire evening. It will be an excuse to wear a beautiful gown and drink champagne. A bit of good fun with a new friend. Please?" She looked up at me from beneath long lashes, her red lips pouted out persuasively.

"There will be plenty of champagne?" I asked, smiling a bit.

Sophia clapped her hands, knowing she'd snared me. "We can bathe in it if you'd like."

"I expect a tub when I arrive," I teased.

She narrowed her eyes at me and wagged a finger. "You will fit right in."

9

Rose Beckingham fit in against Sophia Carden's society friends just fine. Nellie Dennet, however, balked at the opulence of Sophia's home. The delicate crystal chandeliers and champagne flutes, the marble busts mounted on fluted columns around every doorway, the rich tapestries hanging from the walls. Nellie Dennet had never seen such obvious wealth. Even the Beckingham family, both in London and India, didn't display their wealth so garishly. I'd never seen anything like it.

"Rose, I am so thrilled you came," Sophia said when she saw me standing in awe in the entryway. She grabbed my arm and pulled me into the party. "I was worried you'd cancel at the last minute."

The truth was, I'd wanted to send Aseem with my written apologies and hide in my own home all night. However, I also knew I had been handed a rare opportunity to delve into the London art world, which would certainly help my investigation. Also, something about Sophia Carden struck me as odd. The way she had latched on to me at the museum and immediately invited me into her home to meet her friends felt strange. Perhaps, I was judging her friendliness a bit too harshly, but perhaps she was up to something. Either way, I wanted to step into her home and find out for myself.

"Never," I said. "Though, I'd like to be shown to my champagne tub immediately."

Sophia turned back to me, eyebrows pulled together in confusion before she remembered our joke from earlier. A smile cracked across her heart-shaped face. She turned back around and waved her free hand in the air as though trying to be rescued from sea. "Attention everyone, my new friend has arrived!"

The guests milling around the dining room all stopped and turned to me, and I nearly fainted on the spot. The weight of their attention was unbearable.

"This is Rose," she said, graciously skipping over my surname. "Be kind to her. I like her a great deal."

A few well-dressed people nodded at me, but most of them took a moment to peruse my attire—a blue silk dress with silver beading along the neck and hem—and went immediately back to their previous conversations. For this, I was grateful. Sophia excused herself to greet a few other guests, and I took the opportunity to snag a flute of champagne and observe the party.

I'd felt fashionable when I left my house, but suddenly I looked positively dowdy. These women were ornate, each of them like a piece of artwork. One woman was covered head-to-toe in so many beads it was a wonder she could lower her arms without scraping them.

"I acquired one of his latest pieces," the woman said, her hand dancing through the air while she spoke. "Everyone is saying he will be the next big name, so I couldn't resist adding him to my collection."

"His work is nothing more than smears of paint," the man next to her said, shaking his head disapprovingly. "They are grotesque doodles parading around as artistry."

I'd come into the conversation too late to know who they were talking about, but as someone with little knowledge of art, I wouldn't have had an opinion of the work even if I had heard the artist's name.

"It's surrealism, dear," the woman said, patting the man on the arm and shooting a pitying look at the group. "Everyone in Paris is going wild for it."

"Well, Paris can keep their surrealism. The only thing I find surreal about it is that you convinced me to spend so much money on it."

At that, the group laughed, and then continued a rather spirited debate on the validity of the latest styles of art coming out of London and other large cities in Europe.

"The war changed things," another woman said. She wore a plain black dress with a matching hat but was dripping in diamonds and pearls. "Art is no longer a reflection of our world, but an escape. A place where people can forget what we've lost."

"Do you have any idea which painting is being revealed tonight?" another man asked, his hand pressed to the lower back of the woman in the black dress.

"I didn't even know anything was being revealed until I arrived and saw it hanging in the foyer with a big sheet over the top. It's all very dramatic," the first woman said.

"As long as it isn't any of this surrealism nonsense, I don't mind," the man said.

The woman with him once again apologized to the group for the man's behavior, but I was already spinning away from them, headed to the foyer. I hadn't noticed a painting when I'd arrived, but I'd been pulled along into the house pretty quickly once Sophia spotted me. Even though I knew there was little chance the painting being unveiled that night would be 'The Chess Match,' I couldn't help but wonder.

A crowd of people were standing near the painting, playfully lifting the corner of the sheet to aggravate Sophia.

"If any of you unveil this piece before it is time, you'll be banned forever," she shouted with a smile.

The crowd laughed.

"If you didn't want your party of art lovers to expose this painting, perhaps you shouldn't have supplied such a surplus of champagne," a young man in a trim black suit shouted over the crowd.

"You're right, next time it will be a dry party," Sophia shouted back.

The crowd booed and hissed playfully, but Sophia was able to clear them out of the foyer easily enough. She was a slight woman, but her personality was large and commanding. Even I, suspicious as I was of her motives for inviting me, couldn't help but find her charming.

"I hope everyone has been kind to you?" Sophia asked, coming up behind me.

"Perfectly polite." I hitched my thumb over my shoulder. "There will be a painting unveiled later?"

"Not you, too," Sophia said, smiling and rolling her eyes at me. "I'm meant to be a hostess, but I've turned into a guard, it seems. Do I need to worry about you tearing away the sheet and ruining the surprise, as well?"

I shook my head. "No, I would never. I only wonder why it must be a surprise? What is so special about this painting?"

Sophia leaned in, a hand pressed to her mouth. "Nothing, honestly. It is just a bit of fun to make the party more exciting. The guests have been to so many of these benefits, it's nice to add in a new element every once and again. For zest."

I nodded, but my questions were far from answered. How much zest was Sophia Carden looking for? Enough to steal a famous painting and showcase it at a party? I couldn't imagine anyone being willing to do something like that, but I knew remarkably little about Sophia.

She disappeared into the kitchen to scold the cooks for not sending out enough hors d'oeuvres, and I moved in the opposite direction, hoping to explore the home and discover a bit more about my new friend. Most of the party seemed to be stationed in the foyer, the main sitting area and the dining room, meaning the rooms to the right of the foyer were empty.

I stepped into a second sitting room decorated with furniture just as lavish as the first—a tufted velvet sofa with a dark wooden frame, two matching white armchairs, and deep mahogany bookshelves filled to the brim with leather-bound books on either side of a marble fireplace. I tried to imagine Sophia sitting in one of the armchairs, enjoying the quiet of her home with a roaring fire and a good book, but it was impossible to imagine her stationary. Ever since I'd met her, she'd been on the move. The house looked as though it had been decorated with someone else in mind entirely.

In the corner of the sitting room was a roll-top desk with a leather chair in front of it. I could hear the chatter of the party guests floating from the other room, but I was still alone, so I casually walked over to the desk. I ran my finger along the top as though I was simply admiring the wood grain, and then slowly rolled the lid into the upward position. As soon as I opened it, I could see why the lid had been closed. The desk was a mess of mail and papers and ink spills. It was so messy, in fact, that I simply stared at it, unsure where to even begin.

That was when I noticed the corner of a piece of paper sticking out of the center drawer. Ignoring the messy desk altogether, I pulled open the drawer and found a small, handwritten note tucked away inside. Quickly, I read the letter.

THE PAINTING IS HIDDEN *where we discussed. I took a great risk for you and am awaiting my payment. – P.G.*

THE NOTE WASN'T ADDRESSED to anyone in particular, but the initials at the bottom were clear as could be: P.G., the same as the guard I had followed and talked with the day before, Peter Grove. Could the note be in reference to 'The Chess Match'? Had Peter stolen it for someone else in exchange for a payment? Could that someone else be Sophia Carden? She had joked at the museum that perhaps the painting wasn't really out for restoration, but instead had been stolen. Had that been her own private joke? One she didn't anticipate I would understand?

A storm of questions were swirling through my mind when I heard footsteps in the hallway.

"If anyone touches that painting, I swear they will not be invited to the next party." Sophia's voice echoed down the hallway.

As fast as possible, I shoved the note back into the drawer and lowered the top on the desk. I had just finished and was turning around when Sophia strolled into the room, her face flushed from alcohol and excitement.

"There you are," she said, holding out a hand for me. "I've been looking for you."

"I just needed a quiet moment alone. I'm not used to these kinds of parties," I said, making a hasty excuse.

Sophia gave me a strange look somewhere between fondness and amusement, and then ushered me back into the foyer. It didn't seem as though she suspected me of snooping through her belongings, but I couldn't be sure. I hadn't truly suspected her of stealing the painting from the museum, yet it now looked as though there was a strong possibility she had. There was either a good explanation for the letter, or Sophia was a world-class actress.

While I'd been gone, the entirety of the party had congregated in the foyer. The painting was still covered when we returned, which Sophia was pleased about. A grand staircase stood off to the right, leading upstairs, and Sophia took up a position halfway up the stairs so she was near the top corner of the painting.

"Is everyone here?" she asked, shouting into the small crowd below. Everyone played their part by glancing around and nodding, and Sophia clapped her hands together, delighted. "Wonderful."

"Are we finally going to see what's behind this sheet?" A man with a bowtie and bright red hair asked.

A joke about it being a nude portrait of Sophia rumbled amongst the male guests, who were all quite drunk by this point in the evening, but Sophia brushed them off with a stern look and continued.

"The time has come to reveal the painting you all have been begging to see all night," she said to a round of raucous cheers. "However, as this is not my home, I do not feel it is right for me to unveil the painting."

This took me by surprise. Sophia had invited me to the

party and greeted me at the door. And based on the way I'd seen her commanding the cooks and servers earlier in the night, I'd assumed she lived in the house. I hadn't thought for a second I was in a stranger's home. But if the house did not belong to Sophia, that meant the letter I'd found in the desk had been meant for someone else. But who?

I'd chosen a spot near the back of the foyer to avoid the jostling of the drunk party guests, but I instantly regretted my distant position when a figure appeared at the top of the staircase. From what I could see of the man from my place across the room, he had a tall, lean frame and was dressed in an impeccable suit that had clearly been tailored to his exact measurements. His hair was blonde and smoothed to one side of his head. Most of the specifics of his features were hidden in shadow.

"For those of you who do not know, I am Augustus Lockwood," the man said. "Thank you for being my guests for the evening."

The crowd hushed at Augustus' words in a way they never had with Sophia. Everyone seemed mesmerized by his appearance, and I wondered whether I shouldn't recognize his name. Was the man famous in London society? I had never heard of him but considering I had spent the previous ten years in India, that hardly counted for anything.

"I assume we are all here for the same reason—a love of the arts. As someone with ample means, I like to contribute what I can to ensure art is appreciated and accessible to everyone. That is why I have purchased this painting and will be donating it to the museum."

Everyone gasped and clapped as though he had announced his intention to take in the city's homeless. Not wanting to stick out, I joined in, though I still did not truly understand the point of the party. I couldn't understand why Augustus Lockwood would throw a party and then stay upstairs throughout the duration of it, or why his act of charity was being paraded in front of London's elite. I also couldn't understand why people were clapping for a painting they hadn't seen yet.

"Shall we reveal it now?" he asked, looking down at the crowd and then over at an adoring Sophia. She pursed her lips and nodded before looking out at me. I gave her a polite smile and then glanced up to see Augustus Lockwood looking at me, as well. At least, it seemed like he was looking at me. The shadow from the large painting made it difficult to tell.

Augustus reached out over the banister to pull a velvet cord with a matching tassel on the end. I almost laughed at the showmanship of the entire affair. It was truly over the top. But then, in the moment between when Augustus pulled the cord and the sheet dropped away from the painting, a cold panic set in. I'd decided earlier that it was incredibly unlikely that the painting sitting in the foyer was the stolen painting from the museum, however, in those precious seconds, I had my doubts.

I'd found the letter in what I now realized to be Augustus' desk that connected him to Peter Grove and the museum. Perhaps, this society of art lovers really had stolen a famous painting from a museum for a bit of fun. They were wealthy enough to buy themselves out of any serious trouble, I was sure. I had almost convinced myself that my investigation into the stolen painting would be over as soon as the sheet was lowered.

But then, the sheet dropped.

The painting was a beautiful portrait of a woman in a rose garden. It looked like hundreds of other paintings I'd seen in museums. Nothing special or extraordinary. Nothing to do with a chess match.

"*The Rose*," Augustus announced to a chorus of hummed appreciation.

I almost felt disappointed that Augustus Lockwood hadn't revealed himself as the thief. Or, at least, not yet. The letter from Peter Grove proved only that he had procured a painting. Under different circumstances, it certainly would have connected him to the theft. Except, Augustus had just purchased 'The Rose.' I had no way to know whether Peter was referencing 'The Rose' or 'The Chess Match' in the letter. And it seemed there was only one way to know. I'd have to ask one of two people who knew of the letter.

"Isn't it wonderful?" a woman next to me asked, her eyes glassy, whether from alcohol or sheer admiration I couldn't tell.

"Beautiful," I said. "And a lovely gift to bestow to the museum."

"Yes, Augustus is such a benevolent man. Always giving."

"Does he donate often?" I asked.

The woman turned towards me so sharply her pinned curls nearly fell out. "Have you never heard of Augustus Lockwood before?"

I smiled in apology. "I'm new to the city. This is the first party of his I have attended."

She tipped her head back in understanding and then leaned in conspiratorially. "This is the first party he has ever thrown. No one has been here before."

"I thought you knew him well?" I asked, confused.

The woman shook her head. "I know *of* him. Everyone does. But he is rarely in the city, and when he is, he doesn't show his face. Looking at him, I feel like I'm seeing a ghost."

Just then, Augustus Lockwood moved down towards the

bottom of the stairs to answer more questions about the painting, and the woman next to me took off, nearly running over three other people to get to the front of the line.

It seemed strange that such a mysterious figure in the London art scene would choose to show himself at the same time a famous painting was stolen. I decided then that regardless of the strange circumstances by which I'd found myself in Augustus Lockwood's home, I would make the most of my presence there. If he didn't show himself often, then I had to take the opportunity to speak with him.

I joined the rest of the party near the bottom of the stairs, slowly moving closer to him as people either had their questions answered or grew thirsty for more champagne. I was not far from the mysterious man, only a few people blocking my path, when Augustus Lockwood sighed deeply and turned to move up the stairs, talking as he went.

"Thank you for a lovely evening. I will have to gather you all together again soon. Until then, good night."

And before I could protest, Augustus Lockwood had disappeared up the stairs, and the party was over.

10

The evening air sent a chill through me, and I wished I'd thought to bring something warmer than a shawl to cover up with. Still, I took my time with the walk home from Augustus Lockwood's party. The velvety blue sky was dusted with bright stars, and the city was quiet in a way it never was during the day. Anybody who passed me on the sidewalk kept their heads down. It was too late for idle conversation or smiles. Walking at night felt like being perfectly alone in the world, which in that moment, seemed like a good thing.

Life would certainly be less complicated with fewer people. I'd come to London with the express purpose of using Rose's inheritance to track down my long-lost brother. However, I'd become unintentionally attached to Lord and Lady Ashton and their children—though my opinion towards Edward had understandably soured—and that attachment had led me into all kinds of trouble. I'd investigated a murder upon first arriving in London because I believed the Beckingham's driver, George, could have been involved and I didn't want the family to be in danger. And then I'd investigated yet another murder that occurred at their country estate for the same reason, and found myself tangled up with a criminal mastermind. Not to mention, my frequent dabbling in murder investigations had apparently made me a popular freelance detective option. So now, even while planning to move back to New York, I was spending my final days in London at parties full of strangers, hoping to find information about a stolen painting. All of that on top of my own lies about my identity felt overwhelming at times.

Suddenly, my perfect sense of ease began to fade. Thoughts of my current investigation, the strange Augustus Lockwood, and the letter I'd found in his desk began to cloud my mind. Apparently, Augustus Lockwood made very few public appearances, which made the fact that I'd been unable to secure a moment alone with him at the party all the more frustrating. I knew I could talk to Peter Grove again. The first time I'd spoken with him, I had nothing on him more substantial than a slightly suspicious coworker. Now, however, I had seen his initials signed to a letter that discussed moving a painting. Peter had told me that there were people higher up in society than him who deserved my speculation, and perhaps he had been talking about Augustus Lockwood. If I could only talk with him again, I could convince him that I didn't believe he was guilty. That I had seen firsthand how powerful Augustus Lockwood was, and that I understood he may have been coerced or threatened into procuring the painting. Maybe he would confess the truth to me and I could solve one more case before putting this chapter of my life behind me for good and sailing for New York City.

I was nearly home and desperate for bed. The day had been unbelievably long, and I was already daydreaming about drinking the cup of tea Aseem would make me whether I asked for it or not—he really was like a doting parent, at times—and curling up beneath my heavy blankets, when I saw a figure barreling towards me up the street.

The road I walked down was empty now, except for me and the person up ahead, who was hidden in shadows, and a cool dread slipped between my shoulder blades and raised the hair on the back of my neck. The Chess Master had sent someone to accost me in a dark alley once before, and now that he had seen fit to kill Edward, I spent a great deal of energy pushing down the fear that he would come after me next.

The figure, clearly a man, kept his head down, but his long legs moved forward with determination, making longer and longer strides as he neared. I considered turning around and moving in the opposite direction or crossing the street, but I knew it would do no good. I had half a mind to scream, hoping to wake some neighbors and draw attention to the street when the figure looked up and I recognized the brown cap pulled low over his eyes and the tweed jacket that hung from his broad shoulders.

"George," I said, somewhere between a question and a sigh of relief. The panic in my stomach eased away and I inhaled, filling my lungs and exhaling slowly.

George, however, seemed no less ill at ease. He picked up his pace once he saw me, nearly running down the street. When he came close enough and stepped into the light of one of the streetlamps, I noticed how pale he looked, how wide his eyes were. There was a thin sheen of sweat across his face like condensation on a glass.

"George? What is going on?" I asked, touching his shoulder gently.

"I waited inside for a while, Miss Rose," George said,

breathless. "But I couldn't sit anymore. I needed to walk. I've been pacing up and down the block for an hour waiting for you."

"I'm sure that didn't make the neighbors uncomfortable at all," I said, glancing around, imagining little old women peeking out nervously between their curtains. "What is going on, George?"

"I did what you asked," he said, shaking his head. "I followed the man you asked me to follow."

My heart lurched. "What happened? Is everything all right?"

George pulled his hat off, revealing a disheveled mess of hair beneath. He twisted the cap between his hands, his knuckles going white with the effort, and shook his head. "No, Miss."

It was obvious George was in a nervous state, and whatever it was he needed to tell me, the public street was no place for it.

"Come with me," I said, wrapping my arm through his and leading him towards the house. "Let's discuss this inside."

Outside, George had seemed fidgety, but inside, he seemed on the verge of convulsions. His nervous energy filled the sitting room and infected me with an itching just below the surface of my skin.

"Please stop pacing, George. You'll carve a hole in the hardwood. Sit down and tell me what happened," I said, gesturing to the chair across from mine.

George lowered himself into the chair for half a second before standing back up and pacing to the door. "I was following the man you asked me to—Peter Grove. I'd been watching him for a long time, and nothing unusual happened. Honestly, I was bored senseless, and was thinking of asking you when I could stop watching him. All he did was take long walks and smoke cigarettes in the doorway of his building and sit near the front window of his flat. That was the most unusual thing he did, in fact. He would sit in front of that window for hours, watching the street below. Almost like he was looking for someone. Waiting for someone. It made me nervous that he'd notice me watching him, but he never paid me any mind."

"So, why are you so concerned now, then?" I asked. "If all he did was walk and smoke and stare?"

"It's not what Peter Grove did that has me bothered, Miss Rose. It's what...someone else did." George shuddered at the thought, closing his eyes as if trying to fight off a horrible memory.

"George, please," I said, growing impatient. "You have to tell me."

"He was murdered."

The words came out of him so suddenly that I almost wondered whether they hadn't been in my imagination. George had been edging painfully around the truth for a few minutes, so it was a bit of a shock that he just shouted it out that way.

"Peter Grove was murdered?" I clarified.

George nodded and, the truth finally off his chest, dropped down into the chair exhausted.

"What happened exactly? You saw the murder?"

"I did," he said, his eyes fixed on a point on the floor, though I had a feeling he was seeing something entirely different. "Peter Grove was sitting in his window watching the street, like I already told you. He watched as people passed and rarely took his eyes away for more than a minute or so. Well, after a few hours of this, he disappeared inside for ten minutes, which was strange. Or, at least, strange for

Peter Grove. For anyone else, it would have been perfectly normal not to spend hours in their front window."

"Of course," I said, wanting to let George know I understood him, but also to try and instill some sense of urgency in him. The story was coming out of him so slowly that I wanted to shake him until answers tumbled out of his mouth like dice from a cup.

George took a deep breath and continued. "So, he disappeared inside the house for ten minutes and then walked down the front steps. I actually groaned because I couldn't stand the idea of taking another long walk. I tried driving along behind him the first time he went on a walk, but it was too slow of a pace and I blocked the road and drew attention to myself. So, I've walked more in the last two days than ever before."

I was about to plead with George to get to the point and leave out extraneous details when his story began to find its direction again.

"Peter Grove was only two blocks from his house—I was a block behind him—when he disappeared into an alley. I was too far away to tell whether he walked into the alley knowingly or was pulled into it, but he disappeared. I sprinted down the block to catch up to him, and just as I came to the mouth of the alley, there was a deafening bang."

"He was shot," I said, both elated that George had finally made it to the meat of his story, but also horrified that a man I'd just interviewed as a potential thief was now a murder victim.

"Yes," George said, his eyes wide. "I immediately recognized the sound as gunfire and ducked behind a wall. At first, I didn't know who had been shot. I didn't know if Peter Grove had a gun and was shooting at me or if someone else had shot Peter. Or if Peter was in the alley at all. I didn't know anything, but I stood against the brick building, not moving or breathing or making a sound. Just waiting. When I didn't hear anything for a bit, I chanced a look around the corner and saw Mr. Grove lying on his stomach with blood pooling beneath him."

"And the shooter?" I asked, leaning towards him, brow furrowed under the weight of so many questions.

"A shadowy figure was at the end of the alley, but they were gone before I could get a good look," George said. "I'm sorry, Miss Rose. If I hadn't been so afraid, I might have caught a look at him."

The man hung his head in shame and I reached out immediately to comfort him. "No, George. Do not apologize. I would have never forgiven myself if you'd been hurt because of something I asked you to do. I never would have sent you to watch Peter Grove if I thought there was even the slightest chance that you would be harmed. I believed Mr. Grove to be a thief, not mixed up with murderers."

"A thief?" George asked, lifting his head to look at me.

Without revealing any specific details, I informed George that a local institution had hired me to discover who had stolen something of great value from them, and Peter had been a guard at that institution.

"And now he has been murdered," George said. "Perhaps, for knowing too much?"

"That's what I'm beginning to think," I said. The letter I'd found in Augustus Lockwood's home led me to believe Peter had delivered the stolen painting to its next location. He was not the thief, but a cog in the thief's machine. And it seemed as if that thief had decided Peter was too much of a risk to keep around. It was a tactic I was infinitely familiar with. Edward had been murdered in prison as soon as I decided to get more information from him about the Chess Master.

Because the stolen painting was titled "The Chess Match," I'd had suspicions from the beginning that the Chess Master was behind the theft. However, the death of Peter Grove seemed to further confirm this theory. Much like with Edward, somehow the Chess Master had found out I wanted to question Peter Grove a second time, and decided it was not worth the risk. He'd asked one of his many underlings to murder Peter before I could talk with him again.

"Are you going to stay on the case?" George asked.

I looked up at him, pulled from my thoughts. "Of course. Why wouldn't I?"

George's eyes widened in surprise. "Because a man was murdered. It isn't safe, Miss Rose."

"Peter's death means I'm getting close," I said. "The person behind the theft and the murder wouldn't be afraid of me for no reason."

"What are you going to do next, then?"

I hesitated for a moment, not sure if I wanted to get George involved, but relented. It was exhausting keeping so many secrets from George and Aseem. And now that George had witnessed a murder and knew I was involved somehow, it seemed silly not to inform him of my next steps.

"I think my next step should be to try and locate the stolen painting. I have strong reason to believe Peter Grove knew where the painting was being held. Of course, now that he is dead I cannot ask him where it is, but there may be another way to find the information," I said.

"How?" George asked.

"I can break into his house."

George shook his head. "No, Miss. It is too dangerous.

Mr. Grove seemed to think someone was out to get him, based on the way he stared out his window all day, and now he is dead. If you snoop through his home, you could put yourself in the same kind of danger."

I stood up, shaking off the exhaustion from the long day, trying to work up the energy to leave the house again. "I cannot sit back and let a potential lead go to waste. I'm sure the woman living with Mr. Grove will be at the police station right now, meaning the house is likely empty. Now is the time to strike."

I was heading towards the door to grab my coat when George walked past me and then turned to block my path. "I'll come with you."

"No, George," I said, waving him away. "Really, you have done enough. I can't ask you to put yourself in harm's way for me again."

"You don't need to ask me," he said. "I'll do it regardless. You gave me a job when no one else would, and I am grateful for that. This is how I repay you."

I wanted to insist that George stay at the house, but I could tell by the resolute set of his shoulders and the thin line of his mouth that it would do no good. And I was about to shake my head and relent when another voice piped up from behind me.

"I would like to come, as well," Aseem said, his voice quiet, but stern.

He was standing in the doorway wearing white pants and a dark tunic that hung nearly to his knees.

"How long have you been listening?" I asked, narrowing my eyes, but unable to hide my small smile.

He looked up at me, a guilty glint in his eyes that made it clear he had been eavesdropping throughout the entire conversation.

I sighed and looked between the small Indian boy and my middle-aged driver. "I cannot guarantee either of you will be safe. And I cannot guarantee we will not be caught in the act and arrested."

They both nodded once, quickly, and that was that. We were all three off to solve a murder and a robbery.

11

B y the time our unlikely trio made it to Peter's house, the moon was high in the sky. The streets were mostly quiet, except for the occasional hum of music or laughter coming from open windows. Peter's windows, though, were pitch dark. It was obvious no one was inside.

"How are we to get inside?" Aseem asked.

"The front door seems the obvious answer," I said, but George shook his head.

"It is too exposed to the street. Someone could see. There is a window in the back. I noticed it when I first started watching Mr. Grove. I wanted to be sure of all the entrances and exits."

We crept around the building, George leading the way, until we stopped in front of a window no wider than my shoulders.

"This is hardly a window," I said. "I'm not convinced I'll fit through there."

"You won't need to, Miss," Aseem said, slipping his shoes off. "I'll go."

"Absolutely not. No." I crossed my arms and placed my back against the window, blocking it. "I'm not sending you in there alone. You don't even know what you are looking for."

"For anything that can point you towards the location of the stolen painting," Aseem said.

"How did you know it was a painting I'm looking for?" I asked, eyebrows raised in suspicion.

For the second time that night, Aseem looked incredibly guilty, and I realized that the loyal young boy was also quite the sleuth. I would need to be more careful about what I said while he was around. Or rather, while he wasn't around.

"Regardless, I refuse to send in a child to do my illegal bidding."

"I found information for you on the ship, Miss Rose," Aseem said, referring to our time spent together on the *RMS Star of India* when he eavesdropped on some conversations and delivered some crucial information to me. "And I was never once spotted. I can do it again. Easily. Besides, I'm the only one who can fit through the window."

"I can open it," George said, stretching up on his toes to pry the window open. It took a few good blows of his fist before the bottom scraped open with a shrill noise and he was able to push it inside.

I didn't feel good about the decision at all, but it seemed I was overruled. There also didn't seem to be a better option. The front door was a bad idea, especially if Peter Grove's house was being monitored. We didn't have enough time to get in touch with the landlord and create a false narrative of being relatives of the deceased in order to obtain a key. So, I grudgingly stepped aside and watched as George boosted Aseem up into the window.

The boy looked especially young crawling through the small window, his legs scrambling up the grungy brick wall. But after a few seconds, he pulled himself up and disappeared into the dark building.

"Are you all right?" I hissed after not hearing so much as a whisper of sound from inside.

"Fine, Miss," Aseem called.

I shook my head and smiled. The boy really was good at sneaking around.

After a few minutes of loitering in the alleyway, George and I were growing antsy.

"I should go in after him," George said, stretching up to try and see through the window, though it was much too high.

"And how would you get in?" I asked. "We'd be in the same predicament we were when we started."

"What if he can't get back out through the window he went in?" he asked.

"I suspect he would tell us so by shouting through the window. Or, he'd walk through the front door," I said. "Very few people are as suspicious of people coming out of houses as they are of people trying to get into them."

George took a deep breath and leaned back against the concrete. It was clear he and Aseem had become rather fond of one another, and I was surprised I hadn't noticed sooner. I supposed I had been rather busy with the Beckinghams and the drama of Edward becoming a murderer and then the murdered. Apparently, the time the two spent alone in the house had made them friendly, which I thought was nice.

"Coming out," a voice whispered from inside the house.

"Good," George said, positioning himself beneath the

window to catch Aseem, whose face appeared in the window a moment later.

There was no other way for him to get out of the window other than face first, so he balanced his belly across the windowsill for a moment before tipping forward into George's arms. George grabbed him around the ribs and righted him as if he weighed nothing.

"Did you find anything?" I asked after he'd had a moment to rearrange himself.

"Only one thing," Aseem said, holding out his open palm. In it was a rusty old key. "This was sitting in the center of the dining room table when I walked in. I checked it against every lock I could find in the house and it didn't fit anything."

I plucked the key out of his hand and held it up against the dim lamp hanging in the center of the alley. The number 12 was carved in the key quiet prominently, though I hadn't the faintest idea what it could represent. I was about to ask Aseem what else he'd seen, hoping that perhaps there was another clue inside that he hadn't picked up on that could point towards a possible lock for the key, but before I could say anything someone shouted into the alley.

"Stop, thieves!"

We all three turned at the same time to see a large man with a club in his hands running towards us from the mouth of the alley. It was clear the man, probably a neighbor, didn't wish for an explanation, and I didn't have one to give, so we all three ran in the opposite direction as fast as we could.

Aseem and George were faster than I was. Not only did they not have a silk gown slowing them down, but neither of them was wearing kitten heels. So, they reached the end of the alley before I did, and took a right. I could hear the man with the club growing closer, his footsteps pounding against the ground so hard I could practically feel the vibrations, and I knew I had to make a choice. If I followed George and Aseem, the man would follow all three of us and I would be captured. However, if I chose to take a left and run away on my own, the stranger would likely pursue my companions and leave me alone. Or, at least, that's what I hoped. I took a hard left as soon as I reached the street, and ran, arms and legs pumping as fast as they could.

I was too afraid to turn around and see whether the man was following me. Turning around would only slow me down if he was behind me, and even if he wasn't, I wanted to get far away from Peter Grove's house as soon as possible, so I would have been running anyway.

I careened down the empty streets, weaving across the city in the general direction of my house, all the while hoping George and Aseem had managed to make a clean getaway.

I was a few blocks away when I heard footsteps behind me. I couldn't be certain they weren't the echoed sounds of my own hurried steps. But regardless, the sound struck fear into me. The problem was that I was quickly losing steam. The burst of adrenaline that had sustained me for the first few blocks was failing, and I didn't know how much longer I could run. I needed to hide.

Peter Grove lived in a worn-down area of London. The houses were gray and dingy with cracked sidewalks and burnt out streetlamps. Many of the buildings were abandoned. It was into one of these buildings that I ducked when I felt as though my lungs were going to explode inside my chest.

The front doors of the building were glass, but it had long ago been shattered and boarded over with wood that had rotted from years of rain and sun in equal measure. I easily pulled a couple of boards back and slipped through the cracked opening.

I didn't want to stand right next to the door and be waiting there ripe for the taking should someone be following me, so I pressed into the darkness. As my eyes adjusted, I was able to make out long hallways with doors, most of which were hanging off their hinges. It looked as if the building could have been low-income housing prior to the war. Since then, the flats had been left empty and the ceiling was caving in at the rear of the structure.

I stepped into one of the rooms—number 106—and saw a narrow bed buried under ceiling tiles and dust so thick it looked like snow. Otherwise, the room was free of furniture. The rest of the rooms off the hallway maintained a similar theme. One had a dresser in the corner, but all of the drawers had been removed and were nowhere to be found. Another had a chair with three violent looking springs poking up through the faded cushion.

I was in one of the last rooms at the end of the hall, kicking aside a single leather shoe that lay in the doorway, when I heard a scuffling sound near the entrance. Immediately, I tried to convince myself it was an animal. If entering the building had been so easy for me, I could only imagine how easily a rat or stray cat could break inside. When it happened again, however, this time much closer, my nerve began to fail me.

Panic rose like bile in the back of my throat and I fought back a whimper. I was trapped at the end of a long hallway with no way out. There was a set of stairs in the middle of the hallway between the entrance and where I stood, but I was afraid to walk back in the direction of the noise. And even if I wasn't afraid, I wouldn't have dared to venture up them for fear of falling through the rotting wood and losing a leg or my life.

I walked to the back wall where a soot-covered window was punched into the cinderblocks, but no amount of pressing and pulling would budge the swollen frame. Enough light had come through the grimy window that when I turned around, it took my eyes a few moments to adjust back to the darkness. As I blinked, I thought I saw a figure standing in the doorway.

I stumbled backwards, heart racing, hands flailing out in front of me to protect myself. But when I blinked again, the figure was gone and the doorway was clear.

Even though I was alone, I still felt foolish for being so frightened. I had let the abandoned building spook me into seeing things that were not there and turning the normal kinds of building creaks into the footsteps of attackers. Still, I didn't move for a few minutes. I stood against the back wall of the room, eyes trained on the door, too paralyzed with fear to take another step.

Finally, as my fear subsided and I realized the full extent of my cowardice, I stepped away from the wall, brushed the dust from my back, and walked into the hallway.

I was so shocked by the suddenness of everything, that it took me a few seconds to realize there was a bag over my head. Everything had simply gone dark, and it wasn't until I realized how difficult it was to breath that the truth hit me. Panic flooded through me and I kicked out and swiped in every direction, but my attacker must have been a ghost because I was incapable of striking them. After what felt like hours, but was probably only a few minutes, a heaviness dripped into my arms and legs and pressed my head down into my chest, and I stopped fighting.

12

W aking up was like having been thrown unexpectedly into ice cold water, and then breaking through the surface, mouth open, eyes watering, flailing for a life raft and gasping for air. Except I couldn't flail because my arms were tied to the arms of a sturdy wooden chair and my ankles were tied to the chair legs. And I couldn't see because I had a blindfold on. And I couldn't scream because I was much too frightened to scream.

"You're finally awake."

I jumped at the man's voice, and he chuckled. "I'm sorry to have frightened you."

I could hear him moving in even, measured steps, as if walking to the beat of a drum I couldn't hear. The footsteps grew louder, and I tipped back my head enough to catch a glimpse of his shoes as he walked towards me. Expensive leather shoes that immediately gave him away as a man of means. They were not the battered shoes or boots of a working man.

"I'm also sorry to have to bring you here under such

circumstances, but sometimes there is no way around the inevitable."

I tried to focus on the tone of his voice, the cultured accent with a hint of...something else. It was in the way his voice flattened over some of the vowels. I recognized the voice, though I couldn't put my finger on who it belonged to.

"How do you know I wouldn't have come to you on my own?" I asked. It felt bizarre to talk to someone I couldn't see and didn't know, but just sitting quietly in the chair was unbearable. I had to say something.

"Oh, no. That was not my concern, dear," the man said, amusement in his voice. "I have no doubt you would have met me had I asked. The problem is that I can predict your actions only too well. You would have shown up with a plan. I needed this encounter to be unexpected."

"It is certainly that," I said.

He clapped once, the noise echoing through what sounded like an empty room and making me jump again. "See? You are so fun. I have been most amused by this game we've been playing together."

From the moment I'd regained consciousness, I'd suspected that I had been abducted by the Chess Master, but it wasn't until that moment that I was sure.

"The Somerset Adventure was a delight," he said, as though he were talking about an enjoyable weekend of croquet and tea in the country rather than murder. "The moving parts to that plan made it thrilling even for me."

"Moving parts? Do you mean people?" I asked, unable to bite my tongue. "A man was murdered because of you."

"Ah-ah," he said, chastising me as though I were a child. "A man was murdered because of your cousin. Edward Beckingham planned to kill Mr. Matcham whether I chose to provide him with a poison or not. What was I supposed to do? Lose his business? Do you have any idea how much money I would lose if I began turning people away because they wanted to murder someone?"

Listening to the man speak made me feel sick.

"Yes," he continued, his voice dreamlike and airy. "Somerset was fun, but this adventure has been my personal favorite. It was amusing to be in the same room with you rather than observing from afar."

My heart went still in my chest. I was listening with my entire body, afraid to move or breathe too loudly lest I miss the reveal. I had seen the Chess Master face-to-face. We'd stood in the same room together, and I hadn't realized.

"Have you guessed?" he asked. "I know you are trying to remember where you've heard my voice again. Trying to decide how I was able to fool you. Do not take it personally, I've fooled many people. I fooled everyone at the party you attended."

Of course. Augustus Lockwood. The rarely seen, but often talked about star of the London art world.

"There is an Augustus Lockwood, but I am not him," he said, as though reading my mind. "Augustus Lockwood and his wife were out of the country, so it was an easy enough task to gain entry to the house and host a party there. Flash enough fancy food and finery in front of people, and they will believe anything. Of course, it helps to enlist the help of an elegant lady, as well."

I sighed, feeling more and more foolish by the second. "Sophia Carden?"

"An actress. I didn't even bother to catch her real name. She was desperate for money, and didn't ask any questions. She issued the invitations and tracked you down to invite you personally."

"I still don't understand," I said, no longer interested in

keeping up the pretense that I knew what was going on. "Why did you throw the party? Why did you unveil a painting? Why did you steal 'The Chess Match' from the museum? Why do any of these things and risk drawing attention to yourself?"

"Because it was fun, dear Rose. Or should I call you Nellie? I'm torn on which would make you most comfortable," he said, before continuing without waiting for my response. "I like playing games, but I also wanted to get a closer look at you. I wanted to see if you are really the detective people say you are. I left clues for you to find, such as the note in my desk drawer, hoping you'd discover my identity, but you, like everyone else, were blind to my disguise. It is no fault of your own, but I was quite disappointed."

I'd felt like something was off about Sophia and Augustus Lockwood and the entire party, but I hadn't been able to pinpoint why I felt that way. So, I'd let it go. Some detective I was, ignoring my own instincts.

"Tomorrow at midnight, the Chess Match painting will be moved to a location where it will never be recovered," he said, footsteps growing louder once again as he walked towards me. Tap-tap-tap like a heartbeat. "Unfortunately, our game has come to an end."

Despite being bound to a chair and blindfolded, I'd slipped into a bizarre kind of ease while the Chess Master was talking. But suddenly, I was on high alert. Did he plan to kill me now? Had I not proven myself worthy by solving his game? I yanked against the ropes around my wrists and surprisingly, felt them give a bit, loosening enough that I could almost pull my hands free.

"It was lovely to see you, Nellie." The words were whispered at my ear. I could feel his breath against my skin, the hairs on my neck standing tall. And then, the heartbeat began again. Tap-tap-tap. Only this time, the noise grew softer and softer until it was gone and I was alone.

I spent what had to be the next half hour breaking out of the bindings on my wrists. By the time I pulled my hands free, my skin was rubbed raw from the rough rope. I yanked my blindfold off and bent down to untie my ankles.

I still couldn't believe the Chess Master had left me alive. The whole time I was freeing myself, I half-expected one of his minions to burst through the door to end me. The entire experience had left me dazed. I kept thinking of questions I wished I'd asked and things I wished I'd said, but hadn't had the mental capacity to think about while he was standing in front of me.

It just didn't make any sense. Why had he abducted me only to explain himself? Why couldn't he have done it in a note, the same method we'd used for communication up until that point?

When I finally stumbled outside, I saw the sun leaking over the horizon, the sky a pale peachy color that felt much too cheery for the night I'd just had.

13

George and Aseem were huddled over mugs of coffee in the kitchen when I finally made it home. They nearly fainted when I walked through the door.

"Miss Rose!" Aseem cried in an unusual show of emotion. He moved towards me, his bottom lip trembling for a second before he gained control of himself.

"We thought something horrible may have befallen you, Miss," George said, shaking his head as if to clear away cobwebs. "The man at Groves' house didn't follow after us, and by the time Aseem and I realized you weren't running behind us, we were too far away from the starting point to know for sure which way you'd gone. We're so sorry, Miss Rose."

Dark circles hung beneath both servants' bloodshot eyes. Like me, it was clear neither of them had slept.

"You have nothing to apologize for," I said earnestly. "You two went far beyond the duties for which you are paid, and I am forever grateful for your loyalty."

This cheered them considerably. And truthfully, I felt in

that moment as though I didn't deserve either of them. I'd been lucky enough to encounter both men, and I said a silent prayer of thanks for that good fortune.

It was clear how guilty they felt for leaving me behind, so I opted not to tell them where I'd really been all night. Letting them know I'd been captured and held prisoner would do nothing to ease their worries. Instead I told them that after I'd avoided capture by Grove's angry neighbor and made it safely away from our pursuer, I'd gone to check in on Lord and Lady Ashton and, as it was so late, decided to stay the night. George's brow wrinkled and Aseem looked unconvinced, but they didn't ask any questions, so I left it at that.

I excused myself and went up to my room to rest.

After sleeping for a few hours to clear my foggy head, I woke up and looked at the clock above the mantle. It was already almost noon. The painting would be moved at midnight, and the Chess Master had made it seem as if he would disappear with the painting, as well. My opportunity to discover his identity was fading, and I was running out of leads. So, after deliberating long enough to talk myself into and out of the plan three different times, I sent a message to Achilles Prideaux, inviting him to afternoon tea at a local café.

THE CAFÉ WAS a popular one that overlooked the Thames. It was at the corner of a large stone building, ornate sculptures of lions and gargoyles coming off of the sign above the glass doors. Iron tables were set outside along the cobblestone walkway, each one filled with people sharing warm croissants and drinking coffee and laughing with one another. I guessed my reunion with Achilles Prideaux would not look quite so cheerful. We had left things on a rather sour note after I'd told him I would no longer be requiring his services. And I'd been too anxious about the meeting to sit still, so I'd left the house before receiving his written response, meaning I had no idea whether Achilles would show up to the meeting or not.

Before leaving the house, I'd swapped my stained and tattered clothes for a new outfit, opting for a long wool skirt, a white button-down blouse, and a cream cardigan. Unlike the night before, I wanted to be dressed sensibly in case I was to be chased by anyone or forced to snoop around in abandoned buildings. I also rinsed my face twice, reapplied the makeup that only slightly disguised the scar on my cheek, and brushed a fair amount of dust out of my hair. Achilles Prideaux was a world-renowned detective, so I didn't want there to be a single thing about my appearance that would alert him to what I'd really been doing the night before.

Not only would Monsieur Prideaux not approve of my dabbling once again in dangerous situations, but there was also a possibility he would even view me as a rival to his own private investigative work if he found out I was approached by the museum directors. Of course, I knew I didn't stand a chance of becoming a better detective than Achilles, especially since the entire point of the meeting with him was to covertly pick his brain since my own had become rather useless. I needed a fresh set of eyes on the stolen painting case, and his were the best eyes I knew.

I was already sitting at a table pressed against the railing overlooking the murky Thames, a warm cup of coffee held between my fingers, when Achilles Prideaux strode around the corner. He looked handsome as ever, his lean figure cut in a sharp black suit and his hair smoothed back and glossy. Like always, he carried his cane with him, giving him an air of formality. When he saw me, he didn't smile, but I saw his lips twitch. I ached to know the emotion behind the gesture.

I stood to greet him, but Achilles did not offer me a hand to shake. He simply pulled his lips into a flat smile that stretched his thin black mustache and then sat down.

"It is good to see you, Monsieur Prideaux," I said, reclaiming my seat, tucking my skirt beneath my legs. "Thank you for coming."

He nodded. "Good and surprising, Mademoiselle Beckingham. Especially considering you indicated at our last meeting that you did not wish to associate with me any longer."

He'd said it was good to see me, but his tone said otherwise. I knew I'd hurt his feelings when we'd spoken in the cemetery, but I hadn't expected him to hold a grudge for so long. What was I to Achilles Prideaux that he would care about our relationship?

"I was speaking in terms of business, Achilles," I said, trying to bring the conversation down to a more personal level, even though I had truly planned to never see the detective again. "Surely you know we can remain friends? I know our correspondence will suffer once I leave the country soon, but I'd like to try and keep in touch."

The first time I'd met Monsieur Prideaux aboard the *RMS Star of India*, I'd found him to be off-putting and suspected him almost at once of being a murderer. Since then, our relationship had blossomed into a strange kind of friendship. I enjoyed his company and, until recently, it had seemed as though he enjoyed mine. However, my life was filled with too many secrets for me to be on extremely friendly terms with a world-renowned detective. It wouldn't have been long before he puzzled out the truth about my identity and my past. We were only meeting now because I was desperate.

His face registered a guarded kind of interest, one of his eyebrows flicking up. "You are still planning to go to New York with your cousins?"

I nodded. "I am. And while it is still true I'd like to be friends, I must admit this meeting is also to apologize to you for having been so curt at our last meeting. It was a rather stressful time, and I would have hated to leave things with us like that. So, I'm hoping this will be a much nicer farewell meeting so you can remember me fondly."

His lips pressed together, but he said nothing.

"How have you been these days?" I asked, tracing the diamond pattern of the table top with my finger.

"Perfectly well, Mademoiselle," he said, leaning forward to rest one of his elbows on the table. "And yourself? How are you handling the death of your cousin?"

I felt guilty for how little I'd thought about Edward since his death. Even though he had been my family, we had hardly been close. And once he'd tried to kill me, any chance of a relationship had been ruined. But I smiled up at Achilles. "I have been doing much better than my cousins and their parents, I'm sure. I have been giving them their space and trying to occupy myself. Actually, I just attended an art benefit last night. It was quite the party. Very posh. I felt woefully out of place, of course."

"I doubt that," he said. "You seem to fit in wherever you go."

"You are truly too kind, Monsieur Prideaux. I had neither the wardrobe nor the wealth to rival a single person at the party. I might as well have been a pauper. Still, it was very fun. The host of the party unveiled a painting he had recently acquired, and there was talk all evening that it would perhaps be a painting that, according to rumor, has recently gone missing at the art museum."

"He stole it?" Achilles asked, brow furrowed.

I shook my head. "No, he didn't. It was legally purchased, but it did get me thinking about the missing painting from the museum. A sign on the wall says it has been taken out for maintenance purposes, but people are beginning to suspect something more sinister has occurred."

"People do love to suspect," Achilles said, sipping from his own mug and then licking his lips. "Especially about things they know nothing about."

I laughed, but the sound came out high and strained as if someone had their hands around my throat, squeezing tighter and tighter with every second. "I'm sure you are right, but all the talk did get me thinking about art thieves."

"From you, I'd expect nothing less," he said, actually offering me an amused smile. There was a fondness in his eyes that left me feeling flushed, and I looked away.

The sun was high in the sky, reflecting off the water so brightly I had to squint, and a cool breeze rolled in over the Thames. The day was lovely, and sitting there at the table talking with Achilles Prideaux, it was hard to believe that I had been bound to a chair the night before. That I had spoken to the Chess Master and been less than a foot away from him. In some ways, it felt like a dream. However, beneath the cuffs of my cardigan, I knew I bore the red and angry remnants of rope burn that proved it had been all too real.

"While I have you here, I wonder what you know about art thieves," I said as casually as I could.

"I know they like to steal art," he said. "Do you have anything more specific in mind?"

I narrowed my eyes at him playfully to warn him away from making any more sarcastic remarks. "Yes, as a matter of fact, I did. In your experience, what do art thieves do with stolen artwork? It seems dangerous to resell it in the same city where it is stolen, but in the case of the art piece that is rumored to have been stolen, it is quite large. Not something that could be carried around inconspicuously. Where would a thief sell their goods without fear of being captured by the police?"

Achilles squinted off towards the Thames and leaned back in his chair, one arm resting on the metal back. "If the stolen painting was unique, it would be almost impossible to sell in England. The market would be full of undercover officers posing as buyers, hoping to catch the thief. So, the thief or thieves would likely smuggle the painting out of the country first. Going across the channel into France would make the most sense. There are plenty of eager buyers there who would love to have a museum-worthy painting in their private collections."

"So, the thief would need to be well connected in order to smuggle the painting out of the country," I said.

Achilles nodded. "Art thieves are very rarely common criminals. They tend to be more sophisticated, with a small army of people who can assist them."

He began to explain a case he had worked a few years before that bore little similarity to my current case except that it centered on a stolen painting. I tried to listen but my attention was caught by the sound of a ship's horn out on the river. The noise broke through the hum of city life, and everyone turned towards it before carrying on with their conversations, albeit at a slightly louder volume. But my attention stayed trained on the ship. My eyes roamed the deck where crates of goods, probably destined for shipping out of the country, stood in stacks.

Suddenly, the pieces of the puzzle I'd been holding began to form an image in my mind. Achilles said the painting would need to be smuggled out of the country. What better place to hide it than with other cargo aboard a ship?

The letter I'd found in Augustus Lockwood's desk—which had turned out not to be addressed to the real Augustus Lockwood after all, but to the Chess Master—mentioned that the painting had been hidden at a separate location by Peter Grove. And then, Aseem had found the rusty key marked with the number 12 on Peter Grove's table.

If the Chess Master was telling the truth and the painting was set to leave at midnight that same day, then it was probably being stored close to a wharf where it could easily and safely be moved and stowed aboard a boat that night. And if the key at Peter Grove's house was any indication, the painting would be stored near a pier 12. Either that, or in a building numbered 12.

I wanted to jump up immediately and leave to begin researching possible locations for the painting to be stored, but I couldn't risk making Achilles suspicious. So, I tried to keep my face neutral as I internally celebrated the break in the case.

"The thief had kept the painting in his own residence the entire time. He was not a well-connected black-market art dealer like I'd assumed, but an art lover with a small budget," Achilles said with a chuckle.

I laughed too, though I'd miss the majority of the story. "Is there a case the great Achilles Prideaux can't solve?"

Suddenly, his smile wavered for a moment and he

looked at me with a peculiar expression that I didn't quite understand. "That remains to be seen," he said coolly.

I smiled at him for a moment before casting my eyes out to the water. For some reason, it was difficult to look at him for too long. It sent an unfamiliar sensation through my stomach, a kind of nervousness that never seemed to fade regardless of how long we had known one another. "Well, I have loved seeing you again, but I'm afraid I must be off," I said.

"So soon?" he asked.

"I know it was a short visit, but there is much to be done before I leave for New York, and I promised Lady Ashton I would come by to see her and the girls today. They have not been faring too well since news of Edward's murder became public."

He nodded somberly. "I've seen the talk in the newspapers."

I moved to stand up, but Achilles reached across the table and placed his hand on top of mine, stopping me. My heart leapt in my chest and all the strength seemed to zap out of my legs.

"Would you wait just a moment?" he asked. "I have something I'd like to say before you go."

I nodded, incapable of forming words to properly respond to him. The possibilities of what he was about to say felt endless, but I kept imagining him making a declaration of the romantic sort, though I couldn't say why. Achilles had never made it known to me that he enjoyed my company in anything more than a friendly capacity. But still, even the thought of him making a declaration left me feeling aflutter.

"I know you said our business relationship was over, and I respect your feelings. However, that did not lessen my curiosity in the least. I have continued making inquiries into the 'Chess Master' as you have come to know him, and I have made a few rather startling discoveries."

The mention of the Chess Master dampened any spark of excitement inside me. Images of the night before, his shiny shoes on the dusty floor, his cool even tone came rushing back and the urge to flee became almost overwhelming.

"I have taken your advice and given up all attempts to search for that man," I said, boldly lying as I stood up and straightened my skirt. "You do not need to warn me further, Monsieur Prideaux."

"I'm pleased to hear it, but I do still think you should know something," Achilles said.

"I wish I had time to stay and chat more, but I really ought to get going," I said. "I'm already late as it is."

"Rose, please," Achilles said, using my first name, which he had used so rarely in the time we'd known one another. "The man is more dangerous than you know, and I do not believe he will give up contacting you as easily as you think."

"I hear you perfectly, Monsieur Prideaux," I said, waving at him as I began walking away. "Believe me, I will keep my distance from him. Thank you again for meeting me, and I hope to meet you again one day. Goodbye."

With that, I walked down the block at a clipped pace, leaving a stunned Achilles still sitting at the table, his lips moving around words I couldn't hear.

14

I knew it was unfair to ask George and Aseem to accompany me on yet another dangerous mission so soon after our last one had nearly proven fatal. However, the idea of going alone left me paralyzed with fear. For so long, I had investigated by myself, and even when I'd nearly been pushed from the deck of the *RMS Star of India* and held at gunpoint multiple times, I'd never felt as vulnerable as I did when I was bound to a chair by the Chess Master. He had outsmarted me, and there was no way to talk or fight my way out of it. All I could do was sit there and hope he didn't want to kill me. And I would rather risk angering my employees turned friends than get captured again. So, when I returned home, I called a house meeting.

"Before I begin," I said, standing at the end of the dining room table, my hands folded in front of me to stop them fidgeting. "I want you both to know you can refuse me, and I will not hold it against you. There is no danger of you losing your position or being cast to the streets. I know what I am asking is unfair, but I cannot keep from asking."

Both George and Aseem nodded in a solemn under-standing.

"I have reason to believe the stolen item I am searching for is going to be located in a storage facility near a wharf. I believe the key Aseem found last night will open the facility. And I also know for a fact that the item will be moved tonight at midnight."

"And you'd like us to help you find it?" Aseem asked.

I nodded. "I don't feel safe going alone, and I trust the two of you to help me and remain discreet."

"I feel confident in saying we are both flattered by your trust in us, especially after we left you to your own devices last night," George said.

Aseem nodded in agreement. Both of them looked ashamed, and I couldn't stand it.

"I chose to separate from you," I said, reminding them of what I'd said that morning. "I knew it was my best chance of escape. You should be untrusting of me, which is why I'd understand if you chose not to accompany me tonight."

"Speaking for myself now," George continued as though I'd never spoken. "I couldn't rest if I knew you were investigating this alone. I'd be honored to accompany you, Miss Rose."

Before I could thank him, Aseem stood up. "He speaks for both of us. I will come, as well."

I was surprised to feel a stinging behind my eyes. I'd never guessed when I hired George and Aseem that they would become dear friends, and now, cohorts in my schemes. I was touched at the life I'd been so lucky to have acquired. However, I didn't want to turn into a blubbering mess and make the men doubt my constitution, so I swallowed back the emotion with a small cough.

"Thank you both for being so gracious and willing to

step into harm's way. As dusk is falling and darkness will close in soon, we should leave immediately if we have any hope of finding the item before it is moved."

And so, gathering nothing more than the key and our courage, we set off to find the painting.

THE WHARF WAS LARGE, much larger than I'd anticipated. It stretched a long way down the edge of the water and spanned a good bit of the shore. Small structures were built into it for the express purpose of temporarily holding cargo that would be loaded or unloaded from ships docked there. When George, Aseem, and I arrived at the wharf nearest Pier 12, there wasn't a boat in sight.

"We have a few hours until midnight," I said, whispering, even though no one seemed to be around. "But someone could arrive before then to load the stolen goods onto the ship. It would be best for us all to look separately."

Aseem shook his head. "It would be safest if we stayed together."

"I agree," I said. "But unfortunately, we do not have the time. If we want to stop the thief, we need to cover as much area as possible."

"Agreed," George said.

I sent each of them off in a different direction, instructing them to search for any lock that looked like it could be a match for our rusty key. "If you find anything, I will be covering the area closest to the water. Come find me, and we will test the key."

With our plan in place, we split up into the night. I felt fine until I turned a corner and could no longer see George or Aseem. The wooden structures that had seemed so small at first glance, suddenly felt dark and hulking. They cast long shadows across the ground that the lights near the street couldn't penetrate.

I shook off the dark thoughts and tried to focus on my goal. I needed to find where the painting was being held prior to being loaded on the ship. What I would do with the painting when I found it was another question entirely, but I decided I would cross that bridge when I came to it. I crept up to every door I passed, testing the key in the lock even if they didn't look like they'd be a match, just to be certain. It was slow going, but was the only way I could be confident I hadn't missed something.

I had always relied heavily on my instincts. I felt I had an eye for things that were out of place or unusual, but the Chess Master's admission that he had been masquerading as Augustus Lockwood had rattled my confidence. How could I trust my own eyes when they had fallen on the Chess Master and I hadn't realized it? Now, every possibility had to be thoroughly explored before I could be satisfied.

At the end of the row of small storage shacks I'd been searching, and blocking my view of the street, was a large warehouse. The bricks were crumbling and washed white with salt from the brackish water of the Thames. Though the windows were low to the ground, it was impossible to see through them. Something coated the insides of them, obscuring my view, but it was impossible to tell whether it had been purposefully done or was simply grime built up over the years.

I followed the side of the building down towards the water and then walked around the corner. Punched into the back face of the building, breaking up the solid wall of brick, was a single door. I jogged to it and studied the large circular bolt lock just above the handle. The keyhole looked large enough to accommodate the key we'd found on Peter Grove's kitchen table and it was rusty enough that they could be a pair. Excitement and fear coursed through me in equal measure as I lifted the key to the lock and pushed it inside. It slid right in, and my hand shook as I tried to twist it. But it wouldn't budge.

I twisted back and forth, jiggling the key in the lock, but the key refused to turn. Frustrated, I yanked the key out and twisted the handle of the door violently, wishing I had the strength to rip it off. And the handle turned.

I jumped back in surprise, believing for a moment that someone must have opened the door from the other side. However, when no one jumped through the door to attack me and there was no other sound aside from my ragged breathing, I reached out for the door and realized it had been unlocked the entire time. I felt foolish, but after a few deep breaths, I pushed the door inward and stepped into the building.

Dust floated in the air like a light snow, and lay in thick carpets across the cement floor, muffling my footsteps. From the inside, I could see that the windows were coated in dirt and grime that had collected over the years. Light from the street filtered in through the dark panes, and in some places, I could even see through the muck to the shapes out on the wharf.

Collapsed shelving lined the walls and filled the center of the space, but otherwise, the place seemed empty. I didn't see anything that resembled anything like a piece of art or even anything big enough that the artwork could have been hidden inside. I was about to leave and go find George and Aseem, hoping they had found something more substantial than I had, when I noticed something out of the corner of my eye.

Along the side wall was a hallway, the entrance yawning open like a hungry mouth in the dark. I walked towards it. Doors revealed themselves as I moved deeper inside, the darkness lifting enough that I could try the handles. The first two doors I tried were unlocked, but opened into empty stone rooms. The third was locked, but couldn't be opened with my key. But the fourth and final door, the only one set into the opposite wall, looked different from the others. It took me a moment to realize why. It was because the handle, rather than being dust-coated and dingy, was shiny. The handle was free of dust, its tarnished silver reflecting what little light there was. Someone had opened the door recently. Or, at least, more recently than the other doors.

Jitters flowed through me as I walked over to it, the key pinched between my fingers so tightly my knuckles felt like they'd shatter. This door had to be the one. I knew it. The painting I'd been searching for would be just beyond that door.

Suddenly, I felt nervous. Did I really care about a missing painting? Did I really want to get more involved with this case when I was so close to leaving the city and being done with the Chess Master all together? Did I want to make him angry when he had already proven he could outsmart me by abducting me and then letting me live?

Part of me thought it would be best to just walk away. I could tell George and Aseem I hadn't seen anything, that I had been wrong about the painting being hidden here at the wharf, and I'd go home and drink some tea. However, I also couldn't push down the questions burning at the forefront of my mind. Was I right? Was the painting sitting behind the door? Had I solved the case?

I told myself that perhaps I'd just unlock the door and check to be sure I was right, and then I'd decide what to do if the painting was there. But, I knew what I would decide. I'd grab the painting without a second thought and run away. I'd take it back to the museum, solving the case, but also incurring the wrath of the Chess Master.

The key fit into the door perfectly, sliding in without a sound. And when I twisted the key, the tumblers inside the door shifted and fell out of the way until all that was left was to turn the handle and step inside. And when I did, I saw it.

Whoever had left the painting in the room had clearly never expected anyone to find it. A thin sheet was draped over the priceless work of art, falling off at the top corner, but otherwise it was just leaning against the brick wall. No additional security, no measures to protect the paint from the dust that seemed to coat my lungs with every breath.

As I'd predicted, I stumbled towards the painting before I could even process what I was looking at. I bent to pick it up, but it was heavier than I expected. The wooden frame around the painting was thick and ornate, adding at least ten pounds. It scraped across the concrete floor as I tried to get a grip on it, hauling it up under my arm.

The painting was so large that I had to hold it with both hands, forcing me to shuffle sideways down the hallway, taking frequent breaks to regain my grip. When I made it into the main space, I stopped to rotate the frame and then froze at the sound of voices. They were distant and muffled, but hearing anyone on the deserted wharf late at night was a surprise. My eyes roved around the empty room until I spotted two figures pass by one of the grimy windows in the far wall. I followed the two shapes as they passed by the next window and the next, moving closer and closer to the door I'd walked through to get inside. Within thirty seconds, they'd be in the building with me.

If anyone was coming into the building, it had to be for

the painting, simply because there was nothing else in the building worth breaking in for. Unfortunately, the room where the painting had been was the only decent hiding place. The large room was too open, and the only things to hide behind were the empty shelving units that were on the brink of collapse.

There was a double set of doors leading from the front of the building out to the street, but I could tell from where I stood that they were boarded over from the inside, long nails keeping them firmly shut. The only other option would be to escape through one of the windows, but I highly doubted they would be possible to open. It looked like they hadn't been touched in years, and the moist air off the Thames had likely sealed them shut forever.

Still, my options were few. I could either stay where I stood and wait for the inevitable moment when the two men—likely working for the Chess Master, and therefore dangerous—walked through the front door and attacked or killed me. Or, I could do my best to escape.

The second option seemed preferable.

Hefting the painting up against my side, praying I wasn't destroying a priceless work of art, I ran as quickly as its bulky shape and weight would allow, cutting a diagonal across the room to the window furthest from the front door. I leaned the painting against the wall and then searched the window frame for a latch. At the bottom of the window pane, a metal handle jutted out and upward like a bent elbow. I grabbed hold of it and yanked. Immediately, a loud metallic screeching noise filled the room and echoed around the high ceilings. The noise shocked me into stillness for a moment before I returned to tugging. I didn't have any time to waste.

With every tug, I realized the window itself was shifting

in the frame. When the handle was fully pulled free, the entire window would sit perpendicular to the frame, allowing airflow—or a person and a famous painting—in and out on either side. The wooden frame was slightly swollen and paint flecked off into a fine powder with every tiny movement, but the window was actually opening, which was more than I had expected. I just needed enough time to pry it open and get through before the men made it inside.

I leaned back for a moment, just long enough to see them passing by the last window on the side of the building. They would turn the corner in a few seconds, which was good because then I could open the window without fear of them seeing it open. However, it was also not good because as soon as they turned the corner, they would be inside the room a few seconds later.

My heart thundered in my chest, sweat collecting in the hollows of my collarbone and at the base of my neck. My hands felt jittery and cumbersome, but I kept pulling. The window was open enough that I could feel the breeze off the water cooling my feverish skin and taunting me with freedom. My fingers slipped off the metal repeatedly, but I didn't slow down or stop because every tug was another inch of space for me to squeeze through, and every inch mattered.

After a few more tugs, I was able to pull the handle out as far as it would go until the window was completely sideways inside the frame. I could hear the men's voices more clearly as they neared the partially opened door. I had less than five seconds to get out.

Thankful the opening was tall enough for my purpose, I grabbed the painting and slipped it through the window first, my body hanging halfway out of the frame as I leaned the artwork carefully against the side of the building. Then,

I gathered my dress around my knees and stepped up into the window with one foot and then another. I was balancing in the window when I heard the back-door scrape against the concrete floor and the men's voices echo through the now empty building.

"Boss doesn't know what happened to the key," one of the men said. "So, we'll have to break through the door ourselves."

"That won't be a problem," the other man said with a laugh, fist pounding against his open palm.

I wondered how they'd react when they arrived and saw the door to the smaller room open and the painting missing. Would they understand what had happened immediately? Or, would they scream and shout, searching for the thief who had stolen what they had already stolen?

Either way, I didn't want to stick around to find out. As softly as possible, I stepped from the frame onto the ground below, grabbed the painting, and ran away from the building in a low crouch, fleeing into the dark.

15

I kept my eyes on the ground as I ran, focused solely on escaping unseen and not harming the painting. So, when I finally stopped to look up, I had no idea where I was. The entire wharf was a maze of rows of identical storage facilities, and I had no idea where we had entered the wharf from. So, I decided to move towards the only landmark I recognized: the Thames.

Walking along the waterfront holding a stolen painting was beyond dangerous, especially with two men lurking about who desperately wanted that painting. Even if they didn't care about how priceless the art was, they certainly cared about pleasing their boss, and the Chess Master would not be pleased to learn they had allowed the painting to be lost. But I didn't know what else to do. I'd told George and Aseem I would be searching near the water, and if either of them were looking for me, that was where they would go. So, I clung close to the shore, hoping they would come find me soon.

The painting grew heavy in my arms and I wanted to stop walking and take a break, but standing still felt like a death wish. I didn't know the time, but it had to be near midnight. Surely, the boat that was meant to take the painting out of London would be arriving soon, probably bringing with it a good deal of foot traffic. I didn't want to be out in the open when that happened.

As I moved further away from the abandoned building, I began to whisper for George and Aseem, but it felt like shouting into a closet. The sound was swallowed and dampened before it had a chance to get very far, and I knew it wasn't doing any good. As soon as I stopped calling out, I heard footsteps behind me.

For a moment, I thought the even patter of steps was simply the echo of my own, but then their pace quickened. The hair along the back of my neck stood at attention, and my blood whirred in my ears. I had nowhere to hide. The painting was a large load to carry, so I couldn't run very quickly, and even if I could, almost anyone could have outpaced me in my current state.

Just as despair began to set in, the opening of a bridge came into view from behind a thin curtain of fog. The bridge spanned the river at one of its narrowest points, but most importantly, it was tall enough at the center to accommodate steamboats and cargo shipments passing beneath it. Perhaps, if I could make it to that point, I'd be able to see George and Aseem or, at the very least, where George had parked the car. Even if the chances were slim, they had to be better than going back into the maze of the wharf with someone pursuing me. So, I angled towards the bridge, my tired feet carrying me as quickly as they could.

The bridge was steep and my breath came out in labored bursts, the large painting beating against my calf with every step, no doubt leaving a bruise. But I didn't feel any of it. I just needed to reach the highest point of the bridge and then I'd find a way out. I'd reach the top, and everything would be all right.

The haze that hung over the water began to clear up as I moved higher, and as it did, the top of the bridge became visible. I could see the point at which the bridge switched from ascending to descending. I was almost there.

And then, a head appeared at the top of the bridge. The head was bent downward, a hat pulled low over eyes I couldn't see, and as I kept walking and the person continued moving towards me, I could see his fine wool suit and the thick knot of his tie. And then, I saw the gun.

By the time I thought to turn around, the gun was already aimed at me. The man tilted his head back and smiled.

"Miss Rose Beckingham," Augustus Lockwood said with a sneer. Or, the man who had pretended to be Augustus Lockwood, at least. The Chess Master. "It's dangerous for a lady to wander around the city alone so late at night."

My hands clamped down on the painting. I knew I was trapped. I'd heard footsteps back at the wharf and the Chess Master was ahead of me. I'd been cornered into this position, directed here by a plan, and I had a feeling the Chess Master didn't intend for me to escape this time.

Suddenly, his expression became serious. His mouth turned down at the corners, eyes narrowing. "I thought I mentioned at our last meeting that this game is no longer amusing."

"Perhaps, I wasn't done playing," I said, though I had no idea where the words came from. I was terrified, nearly shaking with fear. But somehow, my voice had come out strong and clear.

"If only you had a say," he said, reaching towards me

with the hand not holding the gun, curling his fingers. "Give me the painting."

I knew as soon as the painting was out of my grasp, I was dead. The Chess Master could steal it away from me in a number of ways, but something told me he wouldn't shoot at me while I held it.

"Give me your name," I said, tilting my head to the side. "Don't deals require each party receive an award?"

He laughed. "*You* are not in a position to make deals with *me*. You'd be wise to give me what I demand."

"Oh, of course," I said, voice thick with sarcasm. "You are a powerful man in this city, are you not? An important cog in the criminal realm. The Chess Master."

"Yes," he said, nodding in real amusement. "I heard you'd taken to calling me by that rather colorful moniker. I quite like it, to be honest. I assume you chose it for the chess pieces I sent to you?"

I nodded. He had sent both the pawn and the king around the time of the Somerset murder committed by Edward, making clear from the beginning how he thought of me and himself.

"I've been planning this theft for quite some time," he said, gesturing to the painting still clutched in my hands. "I simply couldn't resist taunting you with the chess pieces, hinting at my upcoming plan to steal the Chess Match painting. It made everything feel so much more exciting. Though, of course, I knew you'd never solve the puzzle. It was simply for my own entertainment."

I'd always assumed he'd stolen the painting because of the chess pieces, but now it seemed as if he had sent the chess pieces because he'd intended to steal the painting. "You are highly concerned with your own entertainment, are you not? Does everything need to amuse you in order to be deemed worthy?"

The Chess Master took a step towards me, a shaft of moonlight hitting his face, showing me the blemishes and lines. We were nearer to one another in that moment than we'd ever been before—excepting the time I'd been blindfolded—and it felt strange to see him so close. In some ways, he felt familiar to me. Like I'd seem him a thousand times before.

He smiled, his face stretching into a thin mask. "You are amusing me now and you are still alive. So, for your sake, you should hope I enjoy being amused."

He would kill me. I could see in his eyes that he would. I had to keep him talking until I could think of another plan. "How did you know my true identity? The first letter you sent, you addressed me by my given name."

"I recall, Nellie," he said, something flashing in his eyes. The way the vowels rolled from his tongue seemed strange, but I couldn't put my finger on why. "It is not difficult for someone like me to procure information."

"But if you knew who I was, why not reveal my secret? Why not blackmail me? Why would you keep the information to yourself and do nothing with it?" I asked.

"Blackmail is boring."

"Not amusing enough for you?" I asked.

He laughed, his chest hitching upwards once as though the laugh were being forced out of him. The movement sparked something in my memory and I tried to bring it forth. It was like digging through a pit of mud in search of a sinking stone. Every swipe seemed to bury the memory deeper and deeper.

"No, not hardly amusing enough," he said. "Rather than blackmailing you, I thought it would be interesting to become friends. However, I knew that would be unlikely. So, I settled on adversaries. Going about my business with you trailing along behind me became a private pleasure of mine. I enjoyed watching you try to uncover my identity and find where I was hiding. It gave everything a vague sense of unrest."

"You weren't afraid I'd uncover your secrets?"

"Not in the slightest."

My pride felt slightly bruised. Apparently, I wasn't the detective I thought I was.

"Why would you want to be my friend?" I asked, genuinely curious. Prior to receiving the Chess Master's first letter, I had done no business with him. I'd solved a couple of murders, but none that he had been involved in. The only connection he had to me was through Edward, but even that was tenuous. It didn't make sense that a man so high in the London criminal scene would want anything at all to do with Nellie Dennet or Rose Beckingham.

The Chess Master took another step closer. The gun that had been aimed at me for the last several minutes began to relax, and my shoulders subconsciously eased down, my hands loosening around the frame. I knew he could kill me at any time, but for the next few minutes, at least, I felt safe.

"The two of us have more in common than you think," he said, tilting his head to the side. His hat slid back further on his head, revealing the smooth plane of his forehead, slight wisps of unruly blonde hair peeking out from beneath it.

"How so?" I asked.

"We are excellent actors," he said. "We can fool people, take on new personas and fit into them easily."

I shook my head. "I'm no actor."

"Did you not fool the doctors and authorities in India?

The direct family members of Rose Beckingham? The assessor of Rose's estate?" he asked.

"I did, but not because of my acting skills. It was because I knew Rose intimately. She was like family to me. A sister. It was easy for me to take on her mannerisms because I had spent so much time with them."

This seemed to bother the Chess Master, though I couldn't understand why. He ruffled at the idea that Rose was like a sister to me, pacing quickly back and forth across the width of the bridge, the gun always pointed ever so slightly in my direction. "Her family took you in as a servant, yes? A paid helper?"

"I was a companion to Rose," I said. "I received a small wage and food and board. It may not have been a traditional family, but it was better than an orphan's life."

"Better than Five Points, no doubt," he said.

As the Chess Master mentioned Five Points, I heard it. It was slight, but noticeable. A slip in his accent. The same one I'd noticed when he'd said my name before. My real name. It was a rounding of the vowels not common amongst the English, a bad habit I'd had to cure myself of through late nights practicing with Rose.

"It's a tall 'O,' Nellie," she'd say, shaking her head. "Your lips need to be stretched long."

The Chess Master hadn't made a tall 'O.' He had a fake accent.

"Have you ever been to Five Points?" I asked.

"Anyone who knows anything about New York has heard of the area," he said.

I moved towards him, the painting shuffling along the ground next to me. "I can't help but notice you didn't answer my question. Have you ever been to Five Points, New York?"

The Chess Master lifted his face and looked at me for

what felt like the first time. His blue eyes burned into mine, saying more than I could comprehend. "What if I have?"

I stared back, unflinching. Whatever was happening between us, I knew it was important. "Then, I'd say it's a small world."

"And getting smaller all the time." He chuckled the same way as before, his chest squeezing tight, the sound bursting out of him in a single jolt. And it hit me.

"Jimmy." Just saying his name nearly brought me to my knees. Suddenly, everything about the man in front of me became familiar. The crooked slope of his shoulders favoring his right side, the way he stood with one foot turned slightly out, as if ready to run at a moment's notice. The shape of his face, round with a pointed chin, that was so like our father's. The pout of his pink lips that were just like our mother's. It felt insane to even believe the man in front of me could be Jimmy, but looking at him, I didn't see how it was possible he could be anyone else.

His posture relaxed at the sound of his name. Jimmy lowered the gun to his side and pulled his mouth into an uneven smile. "Hello, little sister."

16

Whe hen Augustus Lockwood had walked into the party, something about him registered with me. I felt a magnetic pull towards him, and had a hard time dragging my eyes away. I hadn't been able to figure out why, but now I knew. My body recognized him. Even when my conscious mind refused to see the truth because London was so far from New York and because I'd last seen Jimmy in ratty clothes with lanky arms and legs, my subconscious reached out for him.

"It has been a long time," he said, dropping the false English accent entirely. I hated how much his voice felt like home. I hadn't seen him or heard his voice in almost ten years, but as he spoke, it felt as though no time had passed at all. Though, of course, it had. Time had passed and everything had changed.

"You're a criminal," I said.

"I could say the same of you," he said.

I opened my mouth to argue, but Jimmy shook his hand in the air to silence me.

"Stolen anyone's inheritance lately?" he asked, one eyebrow raised.

"That is hardly the same thing," I snapped.

"The law is the law."

"I did it for you," I said, my voice soft, but harsh. "I took on this life and identity so I could use the money to find you."

"And it looks like you've suffered terribly," he said, looking me up and down, admiring my fine clothes and perfectly curled hair.

"You don't know how I've suffered," I said. Immediately, I saw the blood pooled in our childhood home and more of it spattered in the Beckingham's car. I smelled singed flesh and smoke and decay, and I couldn't even tell where I was anymore. The bridge was gone and my mind flashed between Simla and Five Points, between India and America.

"Perhaps, you're right," Jimmy said, bringing me back.

Slowly, the scenes in front of me faded and I was back on the bridge. A soft haze floated above the water and fog blocked out the night sky. It would have been almost peaceful had I not been there with the Chess Master holding a gun. Or, Jimmy. Somehow, with both and neither at the same time.

"What happened?" I asked, my voice breaking around the words. "In New York? When you left? What happened?"

He nodded. "I suppose you deserve to know the truth. You've waited long enough."

I leaned against the railing of the bridge for support, no longer able to maintain any semblance of strength or bravery. I didn't even know if I should be scared. Would Jimmy still kill me? I'd believed him capable of it when he was the Chess Master, but who was he now? The possibilities rolled around in my head, making me dizzy.

"Back in Five Points, I was involved with some bad people. A gang of criminals who had me running errands for them. I was in over my head, but I didn't know how to get out. And, at the time, I didn't want to get out. Criminals ran Five Points, and I was tired of being scared. When I became part of the gang, I wasn't anymore. But our parents found out what I was doing, and they wanted it to stop."

Jimmy's cheeks were flushed, and I couldn't tell whether it was because of embarrassment or shame or another emotion I didn't recognize. It was strange to look at him and think there could be things about him I didn't know. My entire childhood, I'd thought he was my best friend. We told each other everything. It was the reason I never would have believed him capable of murder.

He said, "Mama and Papa didn't want either of us to end up like the other kids who came out of our neighborhood. They wanted an honest life for us, and they knew how much influence I had over you. They knew if they lost me, they'd lose us both. So, they tried to keep me from the gang."

The fog and haze was growing thicker ever minute. I could feel water beading up on my skin, and sensed the stones of the bridge growing more and more slick. Soon, it would begin to rain, but I couldn't bring myself to care. Listening to Jimmy talk about our parents felt like someone was ripping a scar wide open. After our parents died, I didn't have anyone to talk to about it. I lived on the streets and then went to an orphanage. My life was about survival, and I never truly processed the horrible way my parents died. But now, listening to Jimmy talk about their hopes for my future, even just knowing I was standing with someone who knew my parents while they were alive and could talk to me about them, it was enough to make me want to weep.

"You were so little when it all happened, Nellie," Jimmy

continued, looking off over my shoulder as if there was a whole other world beyond me. "I know you probably didn't feel little at the time, but you were blind to much of what was happening around you. And truthfully, it was probably a good thing. If you hadn't been, the gang might have hurt you, too."

"Too?" I asked, the word tumbling off my lips without my permission. "They killed Mama and Papa?"

Jimmy nodded. I could tell by the set of his jaw that thinking about it made him emotional, though I could no longer tell whether that emotion was anger or sadness. Perhaps, I never could.

"It was a warning to anyone else who would try to interfere with their activities. Family or not, you'd be taken out."

"But what about your note?" I asked. "I found it on the floor, but then the Chess Master...you sent me a second piece. You confessed to the murder. It was in your handwriting."

He nodded. "It was the beginning of my confession. When I found the bodies and realized what had happened, I felt so guilty. I knew they were dead because of me, and I wanted to confess. I thought if I confessed to the crime, the police wouldn't go after the gang, and you would be spared. The gang would have no reason to kill you. But as I started writing the words, I couldn't finish. I didn't want you to read the note and believe it. I didn't want you to think of me as a murderer, so I tore the paper up and shoved it into my pocket. I didn't realize until later that a piece of the sentence had been left behind."

"I found it," I said. "I thought you needed my help.

Jimmy's mouth quirked up in a close approximation of a smile and he nodded. "When your French detective friend began poking around about me, it didn't take me long to draw the connection to you. When I heard of the scrap of paper you carried with my handwriting on it I knew it had to be the scrap that I'd been missing."

"If you didn't want me to believe you a murderer, why send me the rest of the note?" I asked. Thinking for even a moment that my brother could have killed our parents and destroyed our family had been heart-wrenching. Unbearable. "How could you have done something like that?"

"Because I didn't want you to search for me, you foolish girl," Jimmy said, throwing his hands into the air. "I thought you would give up. After I left the United States, Jimmy Dennett died. I haven't been Jimmy in a long, long time. I didn't want to have to explain that to you. So, I sent the letter."

I nodded, trying to understand. I wanted to understand so desperately, but I'd spent most of my life wishing I could see Jimmy again, talk to him, have him explain everything to me. My dreams were filled with our reunion, my nightmares with the bodies of our parents. The thought that I was yearning for him all that time and he didn't wish to see me at all made me feel foolish.

"How did Jimmy Dennett die, then?" I asked. "How did you become the Chess Master?"

Jimmy smiled and I hated how proud he looked. How pleased with himself he was. He was proud of what he'd accomplished in the London criminal world. Our parents died trying to stop him from following a dangerous path, but he'd chosen to skip down it gaily. I wanted to slap him.

"When I discovered the police suspected me of our parents' murder, I realized I had to get out of the country. I stowed away aboard the first ship I could sneak aboard and it brought me to London. Here, I ran errands at first, same as I used to in New York. Petty crimes, illegal deals and collecting debts. Over time, however, I worked my way up. Eventually, I was giving out the orders."

"And it was so easy to forget about your old life? To leave everyone behind?"

Jimmy tilted his head to the side, an amused smile spread across his face. "Are you angry because you think I forgot about you? Do you think I stopped caring for you, little sister?"

I hated the patronizing way he talked to me. He used to do the same thing when we were children. I looked away from him, angry that he was right.

"Being a powerful man means you have a lot of resources. I controlled this city, including people who were very good at gathering information." Jimmy leaned forward, hand held to the side of his mouth, and whispered. "I always had someone watching you, Nellie. Always."

My head snapped up.

"From New York to India to London. From the orphanage to the Beckingham's to your current home. I knew where you were and I knew you were safe, Nellie. That was enough for me," he said, smiling. Then, his eyes widened and he reached up and readjusted his hat, eyebrows waggling. "However, when I heard about the attack in Simla, I was saddened to hear of your passing. I mourned you for weeks. Not publicly, of course, but in my own way. And when I heard Rose Beckingham was coming to London, I wanted to see the woman my sister had spent so much time with. So, I was at the docks when the *RMS Star of India* arrived, and I watched as you walked off the ship, looking just as you always had. Except for the scar on your cheek."

My hand moved subconsciously to the dent in my cheek

bone, the rough patch of skin that no amount of powder and rouge could ever truly hide.

"I wanted to tell you then how alike we were. Two kids from Five Points walking amongst London's finest. But I stayed away for your sake and for mine. A family reunion wasn't worth revealing my secrets, and I assumed you felt the same way. Until, I discovered you were looking for me. Then, as you know, I became involved."

The fine mist had turned to small droplets. I could feel rain rolling down my scalp and my neck, flattening my curls to my face. "And you used me to imprison Edward? He almost killed me."

"Of course, that was not my intention," Jimmy said. "You had earned yourself a reputation for solving murders, and I thought you'd be able to put that skill to good use. Did you want Edward to go unpunished for murder?"

"Of course not," I said. "But you allowed him to commit murder. You gave him the poison that would have made it possible for him to get away with it. Why not keep him from becoming a murderer in the first place?"

"We've already discussed this. It was business. I did not rise to my position of power by policing the people who purchase things from me. I provide a good, and what they do with that is up to them," he said. "In Edward's case, he made the mistake of telling me his plan, and I exploited that. I knew you wouldn't be able to resist solving the case, and I was right. You brought him to justice."

"And then you had him killed?" I asked, finally getting to the question I'd wanted to ask since first hearing of Edward's murder. "So I wouldn't discover your identity?"

He laughed. "No, I killed Edward because he owed me money I knew he would never pay and he was liable to inform the police about where he bought the poison. That particular event had nothing at all to do with you."

When I'd received the note in the mail that painted Jimmy as a killer, I hadn't believed it. He couldn't be a murderer. Least of all, the murderer of our parents. How could the boy I'd looked up to my entire childhood, the boy I wanted to be just like, do something like that? And even though it was a relief to know he hadn't killed our parents, he was still a murderer. What he'd said before was right. Jimmy Dennett really was dead.

"Don't look so disappointed, Nellie. Your life will be much easier now that Edward is gone. He barely believed your lies. It would have only been a matter of time before you would have had to take care of him yourself."

"I wouldn't have killed him!" I cried. "We are not as alike as you think."

Jimmy shook his head and said something, but I barely heard him. My focus had been pulled elsewhere. I tilted my head to the side, ears trained towards the portion of bridge behind me.

I heard footsteps.

By the time I realized what was happening, Jimmy had heard the footsteps too. And from his point of view, he'd been able to see who was coming.

Jimmy lifted the gun, the muzzle pointed directly at my chest. The ease he'd slipped into while we were talking was gone. His shoulders were hunched up under his ears, his thin lips pressed together tightly. "Take another step, Prideaux, and I'll kill her."

Prideaux? Achilles was standing behind me? How was he here? How had he known where to find me? And how would I explain this situation to him? Even if I managed to make it out alive, he'd discover the truth. He'd realize my connection to Jimmy before the conversation was over. My life in London was over.

Achilles laughed. It was an unimpressed noise. "You'd kill your own sister, Jimmy?"

My mouth fell open and, forgetting about the gun pointed at me, I turned to see Achilles standing further down on the bridge, his legs wrapped in tendrils of fog. He had a gun pointed at me, as well. Only, it wasn't at me. He was pointing it at Jimmy. When our eyes met, he winked.

17

Achilles Prideaux knew everything.

Or, at least, he knew more than I had before running into Jimmy on the bridge. I supposed, on one hand, I shouldn't have been surprised. He was a world-renowned detective, and Jimmy and I, in Jimmy's own words, were two kids from Five Points. Hardly secret agents capable of outsmarting a trained professional.

But still, I was surprised. How long had Achilles known? I'd seen him only that afternoon at the café and everything had seemed normal. Had he known then? Suddenly, I had a headache.

"It seems we weren't as skillful as we thought," Jimmy said, his breath hot on my neck. He was standing closer to me than he had been a moment ago, and I could feel the circle of the gun pressed into my back. "You let this detective friend of yours get close enough to discover our secrets."

"The police are on their way," Achilles said. "I sent George to fetch them before I came up here looking for the two of you. So, you might as well give it up, Jimmy."

A horn broke through the night, drowning out whatever

else Achilles had been saying. I looked to my right and saw a steamboat approaching, identical plumes of black smoke pouring out of its columns.

"Do you intend to add me as a trophy on your wall, Detective?" Jimmy asked. "I bet you'd love to be known as the man who captured one of London's most elusive criminals."

Achilles shifted his feet, his eyes glancing over at me for a second. He seemed stable, but I could see the concern in his face. Achilles knew a lot of things, but he didn't know how this would end, and he was worried.

"I'd just like to be the man who walks away from this alive. Wouldn't you?" Achilles tapped his cane on the ground—a nervous habit—and it made me want to laugh. He was pointing a gun at my brother, the Chess Master, but he still had his cane in his other hand. Always the gentleman, even when staring death in the face.

"I'll walk away from this in cuffs," Jimmy snapped, and for the first time I could hear his anger. He hadn't expected to get caught. The Chess Master who was always one step ahead had been outplayed. A small part of me was proud of Achilles for showing him up. "Unless, of course, you plan to let me escape," Jimmy continued.

Achilles opened his mouth to say something, but Jimmy kept talking.

"No, of course not. The Famous Detective couldn't do a thing like that. What if word got out? Your reputation would be ruined." He laughed in the way I was so familiar with, the sharp gust of warm air washing over the back of my neck. "The only way I walk out of here a free man is if I kill you both."

"I'm a fast shot," Achilles said, and I could tell it was a

warning. "If you even think about pointing that gun at me, I'll shoot."

"How fast?" Jimmy asked. "I'm not so bad myself. Do you remember shooting at empty cans when we were kids, Nell? I've only gotten better over time."

Hearing Jimmy use the nickname he used to call me as a kid sent a chill down my spine. Even though I knew Monsieur Prideaux already knew my secret, I couldn't help but glance up at him to see his reaction. Achilles' face didn't change, but his fingers tightened around the handle of his gun.

The steamboat was closer now, slicing through the water of the Thames, the bridge vibrating as wave after wave washed up against the stone.

"Turn yourself in, Jimmy," I said, trying to steady my racing heart. "I'll defend you when it comes to our parents. I know you didn't do it, and I'll help make sure you don't get charged for that."

"And ruin your own life?" Jimmy asked. "Because I don't know if you remember, little sister, but you're Rose Beckingham? What would Rose Beckingham know about Jimmy Dennet from Five Points? What would she know about our parents? Unless you want to ruin everything you have going here in London, you won't be able to speak in my defense, and I'll be hanged."

He was right. I'd have to come clean and return Rose's inheritance. I'd never speak to Lord and Lady Ashton or the girls ever again. I'd be a destitute social pariah for the rest of my life. I might even wind up in prison myself.

"It's all right, Nell. I understand," Jimmy said, sounding oddly genuine. "I wouldn't give up everything for me, either. Not if I was you. I haven't been the brother I should have been to you."

Jimmy grabbed my shoulder and spun me towards him, causing Achilles to shout. The Frenchman stepped forward, the gun raised higher, aimed with more conviction. "Don't you touch her, Jimmy," he shouted.

Jimmy glanced at Achilles, but barely paid him any attention. The gun in his hand was still pointed at me, but I looked down and noticed his finger was no longer on the trigger. He didn't plan to shoot me. At least, not yet. His free hand brushed across the top of the wooden frame around the painting, but it was like more of an absent-minded gesture than anything purposeful. He seemed nervous.

"I disappeared when you needed me most, and I'm sorry for that," Jimmy said. "I should have steered clear of trouble the way you did, but I've never been as easily clever as you. Me? I have to work on it every day. But you're a natural. We could have been a fine team if we'd joined forces. We could have taken over all of London."

Distant sirens began to leak onto the bridge, the sounds growing louder with every second. Jimmy stopped and shook his head as though trying to refocus.

"Don't do anything reckless, Jimmy," Achilles said over my shoulder. "The police are almost here. We can all survive this."

Jimmy ignored him, his mouth pulled up into a lopsided smile. "It was nice to see you again, Nell. As each other, I mean. It was nice to catch up. I wish we'd done it sooner."

The steamboat was coming up fast on the bridge and it blasted its horn again, so Jimmy didn't hear me when I asked him what he was doing. I didn't know him as well as I once did, but I could see the sadness in his eyes, and I didn't understand it.

Was he going to kill me? Did he already regret what he was about to do? Because we both knew killing me and

Monsieur Prideaux was Jimmy's only chance of escaping with his freedom intact.

Jimmy looked at me, his blue eyes clear. "Goodbye, Nellie."

With one swift movement, he stepped away from me, and threw his weight over the rail of the bridge. I watched it happen, but the reality didn't hit me until I heard the splash in the water below.

I ran to the edge of the bridge, but Achilles was already there, grabbing my arms.

"Don't look," he said, though I didn't understand why.

And then I saw the steamboat. It was directly under the bridge, exactly where Jimmy had fallen. The water around it was white and foamy, churning violently. No one could have survived being plowed over by it.

18

A chilles spoke with the police when they arrived, sparing me from rehashing the details. He explained what happened with Jimmy on the bridge—though, he didn't use Jimmy's name—and soon the authorities set out in small boats to search the river.

"Are you all right?" Achilles asked me once he'd finished with the police. He draped his wool suit jacket over my shoulders and I tugged it around myself, grateful for the warmth.

"I'm unharmed," I said, which was as close to the truth as I could get in that moment.

The reality that my brother was dead came with a strange mix of emotions. On one hand, there was sadness. But it wasn't for the Jimmy I'd seen on the bridge. Rather, I was sad for the Jimmy I'd known in New York. For the older brother I'd grown up with who had been taken away from me far too soon.

On the other hand, I was glad the Chess Master was gone. The shadowy streets of London felt immediately safer once he'd jumped from the bridge into the dark waters below.

Achilles took the painting from me without asking a single question about why I had it or where it had come from. For all I knew, he already knew that information, but just the same, I appreciated him not bringing it up.

We walked down the bridge and back onto the wharf, Achilles leading us through the maze of small buildings until we were on the sidewalk that ran along the empty street. It felt strange to be back in the city so quickly. The wharf had felt completely isolated from London, like another world entirely.

"How did you know where to find me?" I asked.

Achilles looked at me out of the corner of his eye. "I followed you once you left the café."

I turned to him, my eyes narrowed, and he shrugged. "It may have been an invasion of privacy, but you benefitted greatly from it, don't you think?"

When I reluctantly nodded, he continued. "I grew concerned when you didn't come out of the wharf with George and Aseem, so I gave up my cover and asked George where you were. He said he didn't know, so I came looking. When I saw you at the top of the bridge with a shadowy figure, it didn't take much sleuthing to realize you were in trouble."

"Well, I appreciate you showing up when you did," I said, wondering what would have happened if he hadn't. Would Jimmy have killed me to get the painting? Would he have kidnapped me? Hundreds of possibilities played out in my mind as we walked, very few of them ending happily.

"You are sure everything is all right?" Achilles asked again, breaking the silence.

He was looking down at me with concern in his eyes, his brows pulled together.

I nodded. "As badly as everything ended, I'm glad I got to see him again. There hasn't been a day in ten years that I didn't wonder what happened to him, where he was, if he was alive. Even if things didn't turn out the way I hoped, I'm glad my questions were answered. I'm glad I understand everything."

As I said the words, I realized I didn't understand everything at all. In fact, I had a thousand more questions.

Achilles laughed before I could say anything. "You wear your emotions on your face, Rose. So, before you even ask, that is how I knew you were hiding a secret."

"How long have you known?" I asked.

"I discovered the truth in part when we met on the boat from India."

My eyes widened. "You knew from the very start?"

He nodded, his mouth tipping up at one corner, proud of himself. "Your accent is very good, but not perfect. I heard you slip up a few times. And I do not mean this as an insult, but you lacked the manners of a wealthy woman. You were meek and quiet in crowds, always watching and observing. I didn't know exactly who you were, but I knew you were not Rose Beckingham."

"Why didn't you say anything?" I asked. "Why haven't you said anything all this time?"

"I planned on mentioning it at the start, but then I discovered who you were. You weren't malicious. You didn't want to bring anyone harm. And really, what harm were you doing by stealing a dead woman's inheritance? I decided I would let you tell me in your own time, should you choose to do so."

"I'm sorry to say this, Achilles, but I didn't plan to tell

you," I said, cheeks flushing with shame. "I was going to leave London and never return."

He nodded, his eyes downcast. "I know."

"And that doesn't change your opinion of me at all?" I asked.

"It simply reinforces what I already knew," he said with a sad smile. "You are stubborn and resilient and loyal, even if that loyalty is to a family that is not truly your own. You would have gone with the Beckingham girls to New York and looked after them as long as Lady Ashton needed you to."

"And I still plan to."

He turned to me, and for the first time, Achilles Prideaux looked completely perplexed. "You are?"

I nodded. "Why wouldn't I?"

His hands gestured wildly and then fell at his sides. "Because you've found your brother. You completed the goal you set out to achieve. From here on out, living as Rose Beckingham would be a choice, not a matter of necessity."

I knew he was right. Moving forward, I would be living as Rose because I enjoyed it, not because it was necessary. However, wasn't that all right? Nellie Dennet didn't have a family. Her brother and parents were dead. But Rose Beckingham had an aunt and uncle who doted on her and two cousins she viewed as sisters. Wasn't that better than nothing? Wasn't a fake Rose better than the knowledge that Rose had died in the attack in Simla along with her parents?

I wanted to say that I was doing the Beckinghams a favor by keeping up the lie, but I wasn't certain anymore. Would it be better for them to know the truth now and have time to mourn rather than discover it accidentally years later?

"Nellie," Achilles said softly, reaching out for my hand and clutching it tightly in his own. It was the first time he'd ever said my real name and my breath caught in my throat like a stone. "You do not need to continue being someone you are not. I haven't betrayed your secret thus far, and should you choose to continue living as Rose, I would never tell anyone. However, it is only a matter of time before you make a mistake. Before you do or say something that the Beckinghams can't brush away. Before they discover the truth."

"They haven't discovered anything yet," I said, trying to defend myself, though I knew it was weak.

"You are new to their home and Edward was charged with murder and then murdered himself. Life has been far from easy for them. But once things settle down, don't you think they will begin to notice the ways in which you are different from the girl they knew? Do you not think they'll realize how little you know about the real Rose's life in London? And don't you think your deception will cause them great pain?"

I pulled my hand from his grasp and turned away. I'd had all of these thoughts a thousand times before, but when they were only in my head, I'd been able to dismiss them rather easily. But with Achilles staring at me, his dark eyes imploring me for an answer, I realized I did not have one. Or, at least, not an answer I liked.

"I know it is not easy to admit, but your time in London is running out. Soon, the truth will come out and not only will you have to face the Beckinghams, but you will likely be imprisoned because of the inheritance you stole."

Panic rose up inside of me and bubbled out. "And how would that change if I come clean now rather than let the lie unravel naturally? Do you think the authorities would have mercy on me and spare me prison? Because I do not think so."

Achilles moved to stand in front of me, bending low to catch my eye, and shook his head. "You could come with me."

"Come with you?"

"I'm set to leave England soon. A government minister in Morocco has hired me to investigate a delicate case of espionage, and I'd like you to accompany me as a partner."

I laughed, but there was no humor behind it. "Surely, the world-renowned Achilles Prideaux does not need a partner. If this is your way of extending me charity, I beg you not to. You have done me a great kindness by maintaining my secret. You owe me no more than that."

"This isn't about what is owed to you," he said, standing straight and looking off towards the water, his jaw set. His lips tightened, and I could tell he was trying to find the right words to say what he was thinking. "Will you permit me to be rather bold?" He turned back to me, and I could see a hint of blush rising up in his tan skin.

I said, "After the day I've had, I can't promise I will be receptive, but you can say what you'd like."

It wasn't the answer he'd been hoping for. I'd never seen Monsieur Prideaux so nervous. His hands were folded together on top of his cane, knuckles white from clutching it so hard. He kept looking down periodically at the ground, unable to hold my gaze for more than a second or two at a time.

"By my profession alone, it is obvious I consider myself adept at reading the emotions and motivations of others," he began with a long exhale. "However, there are certain areas where all men, and women, I suppose, are blind. We cannot see past our own emotions and experiences in order to view the full picture. So, if that is the case here and I have woefully misread the situation, I pray you will stop me once you begin to understand my meaning."

I shook my head. "At the moment, I wonder if I'll ever understand your meaning. Please, Monsieur Prideaux, speak clearly. You will find no judgment from me."

He lifted one of his hands from his cane and reached out for me, grasping my fingers within his own, his dark eyebrows furrowed with emotion. "But you see, it is your judgment I fear the most in this matter."

Perhaps, if I hadn't been so exhausted in the moment, it wouldn't have taken me so long to understand Achilles' meaning. Or, perhaps, as Achilles said, there were some areas where all people were blind, unable to see past their own emotions and experiences. Whatever the cause, I did not see the picture Achilles was painting in front of me until it was nearly finished, and even then, I wasn't sure I'd inter-preted it correctly.

"I first saw you across the dining room of the RMS Star of India. You wore a burgundy gown with gold detailing that was positively radiant. The color suited you perfectly, but even in a drab gray bag, you would have shined," he said, smiling softly, his lips twitching at the sides with nervous-ness. "As a detective, I make it a habit to know about those who surround me. Prior to boarding the ship, I gained access to the full list of passengers and I recognized your name from the papers. I knew of the extremist attack and the government minister and his wife who were killed, their only daughter surviving."

I swallowed, still not accustomed to someone knowing my secret.

"I intended to speak with you, extend my sympathies, and make myself available to you for any assistance you should require while aboard the ship—I make it a habit to acquaint myself with powerful people—but then I heard your voice. The accent, while impressive, was not perfect. There was a layer of something there that would not have been picked up from extended time spent in either London or Bombay, and I began to suspect you were not who you said you were. However, even as a man propelled through life by curiosity, the curiosity of your accent was not why I remained close to you."

"Then, why did you?" I asked, eyes feeling suddenly heavy. How long had it been since I'd slept a full night?

"Because I believed you to be one of the most beautiful women I'd ever seen," he said in a single breath, refusing to break eye contact with me as he spoke. "And as time went on, I saw that we shared many similar motivations. Both curious, both questioning. Our personalities aligned in so many ways, which is one of several reasons I believe you hated me so much when we first met. We were too alike. The others being that I made myself a bit of a nuisance."

He laughed, shaking his head at a memory.

"I feel I have said too much when it can all be summed up in a few words: I have been attracted to you from the start, Nellie. And the feelings have only grown. I sense you may feel the same way, and if you do, you should come with me. I believe our future together could be bright, but I fear for what your future in London will look like. And believe me, the only person I am doing a favor by making this offer is myself."

Attraction. Hadn't I thought Achilles to be a handsome man the first time I'd seen him? Yes, certainly, but what did that account for in the grand scheme of things? I'd also come to think of him as a rather trusted friend—even though I hadn't trusted him with the full truth of my own identity. Did those two facts together mean we could have a bright future? I didn't feel capable of deciding. My mind was muddled with exhaustion and too many emotions to number were overwhelming me. Making a big life decision in that moment would have been impossible.

Not to mention, Achilles couldn't possibly understand what he was asking me. He wanted to run away with me, but he had no clue who I was. His interactions had been with Rose Beckingham. Stylish Rose in her fancy clothes and her nearly perfect accent. He didn't know Nellie Dennet. Not really. Not enough to be sure we could be happy together.

A muted kind of hysteria bubbled out of me in a laugh and I shook my head. "You flatter me, Achilles. Or, rather, you flatter Rose. I think. You know, I can't be sure. One or the other of us inside this body is flattered, but I need a good night's sleep before I can decide which."

Hurt flashed across his face, his lips twisting to the side. "As I said before, I consider myself adept at reading the emotions and motivations of others, and it is clear to me what yours are, Mademoiselle Beckingham. I trust you can find your way home?"

I nodded once, and Achilles was gone, striding down the sidewalk, head held high, cane slapping against the cement with every step. I was relieved to finally be alone, to have a moment to breathe, but strangely, I was also fighting the urge to call him back to me. Once he turned the corner and disappeared, I stared up at the sky, took a deep breath, and walked home.

19

"I heard news of an incident on a bridge near the Thames, and there were whisperings of a stolen painting, but nothing could be confirmed. As you know, we didn't report the stolen painting to the police, and oh, how I regretted it," Henry Branwell said, wiping a hand across his sweating forehead. Being a head member on the board of directors for a museum was apparently very stressful work, because it looked as though Henry hadn't slept in days. "It was difficult to get a clear picture of what had occurred on the bridge from the scant articles I read, but I felt certain of one thing: the painting was gone forever. Yet, here you stand."

He gestured to me with two outstretched hands, a smile spread across his face. The painting, which he had grabbed from me the moment I'd walked through the door of his office at the museum, was leaning against the side of his desk and he kept glancing at it out of the corner of his eye, as if to be certain it was still there.

"The museum directors and myself extend our deepest gratitude to you, Miss Beckingham. You clearly went above and beyond what I ever would have expected to retrieve this masterpiece for us, and we can never truly repay you."

I smiled and nodded, not wanting to tell Mr. Branwell that my desire to retrieve the painting had been secondary to my desire to capture the Chess Master in action. In the end, though, it didn't matter. Mr. Branwell had been correct. The museum truly couldn't repay me. As it turned out, there was no room in the museum budget to hire a professional investigator, which was why my name had entered the running at all.

"You may come and enjoy the museum free of charge as often as you'd like," he said enthusiastically. "And we would be happy to place your name on the official list of donors, as well. That is a high honor, I assure you."

"Thank you, Mr. Branwell. I'm so relieved I did not risk my life for nothing."

If Henry Branwell caught on to my less than subtle sarcasm, he did not reveal it. He was all smiles as he led me from the museum, stopping at the threshold and waving as I walked down the stone steps.

Honestly, I didn't care about the money. Taking on the stolen painting case had merely been a way to make the little time I had remaining in London pass more quickly. And, in that regard, it had been a roaring success. Catherine, Alice, and I were scheduled to set sail in a few days and having been distracted with tracking down the painting and the Chess Master, I had a thousand things left to do to prepare for my extended and indefinite adventure.

"ROSE, we leave in a few days. How can you not have even

prepared your home yet?" Catherine asked as she helped me sort through my wardrobe.

It was astonishing that I had come to London with a single steamer trunk, yet I had managed to amass so many clothes since. Catherine, I was sure, didn't notice. I had seen her wardrobe, and it was twice the size of mine. In fact, she probably thought mine was far below average.

To help me pack, she'd worn a pale pink tea gown that flowed across her hips and stopped mid-calf with a matching pair of pink and white oxford heels. I was wearing a gray wool skirt and a white blouse like a school teacher.

"I've been busy with other things," I said, not wanting her to know the truth of what I'd really been busy doing. Luckily, my name had remained out of the papers even when articles began to appear regarding the disappearance and likely death of an anonymous criminal who had been notorious to the London police. I suspected Achilles had something to do with this, but I couldn't be sure as I hadn't spoken to him or seen him in several days. I rather doubted I'd ever see him again. A fact I couldn't pin down with a single emotion.

"I have also been busy, but I've been packed for ten days. Alice has been packed for six. We are living out of our steamer trunks," she snapped. And then she sighed. "I'm sorry, Rose. Forgive me. I haven't quite been myself."

I wanted to tell Catherine that she seemed perfectly like herself to me. She had always been short tempered, but I understood what she meant.

"Of course, you haven't," I said, turning towards her and placing a hand on her shoulder. "You have suffered a great loss and your life is being tossed upside down. I'm surprised you have managed to be this calm."

She bit her bottom lip, and her eyes looked suddenly watery.

"Everything will be all right, though," I said, not knowing what else to say.

"You don't have to come with us."

I dropped my hand, surprised. "What? Do you not want me to go?"

"Oh, no!" she said, scrambling to make herself clear. "Of course, Alice and I would be happy to have you accompany us to New York. More than happy. You are family and quite dear to both of us."

I nodded, relieved, and went back to folding clothes. "All right, then why are we discussing this? I promised I'd accompany you, and I will."

"I know you did, and that is exactly why I want to make it clear that we do not need you to come with us."

"I don't understand."

"Rose," Catherine said, reaching for my hands and holding onto them tightly. "You have also suffered a terrible loss. And your life has also been tossed upside down. My tragedy is my own, and I would never forgive myself if I allowed it to add to your burden."

I waved her away. "Nonsense."

"Not nonsense," she said sharply. "You never think of yourself, Rose. You are constantly thinking of everyone else, and I wonder how you have dealt with the tragedy of your parents' deaths. I didn't think much of it before because I had never experienced such a loss. I had no understanding of the kind of turmoil it can throw a person into. But now, having experienced the loss of my brother, I wonder at how much worse it must have been for you. Edward was a murderer, doomed to spend his days in prison if he wasn't executed for his crimes. But your parents were innocent people. You had the promise of an entire lifetime to spend with them, and they were horribly snatched from you. Certainly, that kind of shock requires months, even years, of grieving. Yet, I've seen you grieve so little. I know you must, but I haven't seen it, and I worry that uprooting your life once again to accompany my sister and me to New York is unfair to you."

I had rarely seen Catherine speak so passionately. Her cheeks were red from the effort and when she finished, she placed a hand to her sternum and took a breath. I felt like I could be sick. Catherine was so concerned about me, worrying how I was dealing with the loss of my parents without realizing that I hadn't lost my parents at all. Or, at least, not as recently as she thought. I hadn't been grieving as anyone would expect a daughter to grieve because, as much as I loved the Beckinghams, they weren't my parents. Achilles' offer flashed in my mind.

Had he been right? Would my lies tumble down around me over time? I had thought I was fooling everyone, but Catherine, as self-centered and narcissistic as she could be, had noticed that I was not as sad as she would expect. So, who else had noticed something strange about me, but been hesitant to mention it? How many people had doubts about my identity, and how long would it be before they came out?

"Of course," Catherine continued. "I would never turn you away. Having a familiar face in New York would be a great help to Alice and me, but do not come out of duty to us. You must do what is right for you, and I cannot tell you what that is."

"Thank you for thinking of me," I said, finally. "I mean that. I feel so lucky to have all of you in my life, and perhaps that is why I have not been grieving the way anyone would expect. Because, although I did lose my parents, I gained another family. You all have seen me through these difficult months and made my pain tolerable, and because of that, I feel it is no burden at all to go with you to New York."

Catherine nodded. "As I said, it is your decision to make. I only want you to know that it is a decision. You may choose to go or stay, and no one would fault you."

We smiled at one another, and then slipped back into our preparations. There wasn't much else to be said, though there was plenty to think about. Namely, how long my rouse would last, and, now that I had found Jimmy, whether it *should* last.

20

C atherine did not mention my going to New York again, but I could feel her eyes on me as we continued with preparations in the following days. After staying away on my aunt's orders, I finally joined Lord and Lady Ashton for dinner two nights before we were set to depart for the United States.

"I cannot believe my girls will be gone," my aunt said, holding a napkin to her endlessly dripping nose. The skin just above her lip was permanently red from all of the wiping she had done in the weeks since Edward's arrest and murder. She had also grown quite gaunt. Hollows had settled beneath her cheek bones and her eyes were ringed in blue that had not been there before. I had always thought Lady Ashton looked quite young for her age, but she had aged significantly since Edward's death, and I wondered how much older she would look when her daughters left her, as well.

"And you, too, Rose. Of course," she said, giving me a sad smile. "The house will be so quiet when you are all gone."

"Are you forgetting about me, dear?" Lord Ashton asked.

Lady Ashton laughed. "Yes, because you are so fond of conversation. I will have to take up with the cooks if I want any good idle chit chat."

Where Lady Ashton was visibly shaken by everything that had befallen her family, Lord Ashton looked as unwavering as ever. He sat tall in his chair, his face tan and full, shoulders wide. I knew the death of his son had hit him hard. Especially hard, even, considering Edward had been his only son and male heir. Not to mention, the way his connections to high society had begun to disintegrate. Many of the family's friends had disappeared once word of Edward's crime began spreading in the papers, and his funeral had been quite poorly attended, as no one wanted to be associated with a murderer. Still, Lord Ashton didn't express any of this pain in a way I could see, not in front of me, at least. Neither did he complain of the family's waning financial circumstances or how they could have used my inheritance—if only I didn't stand in the way.

"Begin talking to the servants too much and they may demand a raise in their wages," he warned, winking at his wife when she narrowed her eyes at him.

Lady Ashton suddenly turned serious. "We need to hire a new cook, in fact. Did you know our cook left us, Rose?"

I shook my head. "No, I hadn't heard."

"No one wants to work with us now that..." her voice trailed off.

"Now that we are related to a murderer," Lord Ashton finished, his fist clenching tightly around his fork. "A few children ran up and knocked on our door the other day. When the maid went to answer it, they ran away in terror, screaming about being murdered."

"That's horrible," I said, meaning it. "People can be so cruel."

"And parents are raising their children to have no respect. We are grieving, but no one seems to mind that. The newspapers just want another story to help them sell copies, and people want something to talk about over afternoon tea when the conversation lags."

Lord Ashton's face turned a nasty shade of red and I was surprised by his emotional outburst, considering how calm he had been only moments before.

Lady Ashton reached out and patted his hand, and something inside of him seemed to unclench. He smiled at her, and I was immensely glad that they had one another. It made me believe that, despite everything, they would be all right in the end.

"I wish I had been there more for all of you in the days after he passed," I said, still nervous to mention Edward by name in their presence. "I feel terrible that you had to go through something so traumatic on your own."

"I instructed you to stay away," Lady Ashton said, eyes wide. "Do not feel guilty for that. I wanted to spare you our troubles."

"I did not spare you mine," I said, voice breaking around the words. I coughed, trying to clear the emotion from my throat. "I suffered a loss and you all took me in without a second thought. You gave me a home and a family, and I should have disobeyed your orders and been here with you."

Lady Ashton pushed her chair away from the table and moved to stand behind me, her arm draped across my shoulders. "No one here holds any grudges and we understand perfectly well. So, no more discussing it."

I smiled at her, and we ate the rest of dinner without mentioning the many different things that would bring everyone at the table varying degrees of pain. We discussed the weather and the wood grain of the table and our favorite London fashions, moving from topic to topic as if walking through a minefield, cautious of every step.

When dinner was finished, we moved to the sitting room, and sipping on tea, I brought up the one topic I'd been planning to discuss with Lord and Lady Ashton for several days but hadn't found the right time. I'd finally realized there would be no right time.

Lady Ashton was perched on the end of the couch, holding her cup and saucer, but drinking nothing, her eyes fixed blankly on a spot on the rug.

"I don't mean to put you on the spot, and please stop me if I am crossing a line," I began, setting my tea down on the small table between us. "But I have a proposition that I believe may benefit all of us."

Lady Ashton perked up and Lord Ashton didn't move save for his eyebrows, which quirked up slightly.

"I'm happy to go with Catherine and Alice to New York, but I am sad to leave the home I've just made for myself here in London," I said.

Lady Ashton interrupted me. "Of course, it was wrong of me to ask so much of you. I shouldn't have—"

"I'm not saying I don't want to go," I said, talking over her. "I'm only worried about the members of my household."

My aunt turned her head to the side, eyebrows drawn together.

"Aseem and George," I reminded her.

"Ah, yes, of course," she said, nodding. "Your man servant and driver."

"Yes, Aseem and George. They have been the most loyal employees anyone could ever hope to have, but I don't suspect I will be coming back to London for quite a long time. At first, I thought I would keep the house and allow Aseem and George to live in it, but now I am planning to sell. I'm happy with my decision, but heartbroken to think they would be left without jobs."

At this point, Lady Ashton had begun to guess what I was asking, and I could see the hesitation cloud her face. She pulled her lips tight and took a restrained sip of what was certainly cold tea. "That is a shame."

"Yes, it is," I said, impassioned. "It is the only hesitation I have about going to New York, and I have been thinking of some way that I could ease my mind and help their situation."

She hummed. "Uhm-hmh."

"And so, I of course, thought of the two of you. Aunt and Uncle, would you ever consider hiring the members of my household staff as your own? They both come with my highest recommendation. Though, you already know George."

Lord Ashton finally spoke up. "Yes, we do. And, if you remember, we dismissed him. In fact, we strongly discouraged you from hiring him."

I nodded. "I know that George may have lied to you about his past, but he has committed no crimes while employed by your house or mine." I decided that breaking into the home of a potential art thief didn't count as a crime.

"The scandal we are already dealing with because of Edward's...actions," Lady Ashton said, shaking her head. "I don't know that we could take any more. And we simply don't have a place for Aseem. We have enough servants."

"He is a wonderful cook," I added. "Well, he is learning, at least."

"I'm sorry, Rose, but I don't think we can help you," she said.

"But you have not replaced George yet, correct?"

They both nodded in assent. And Catherine sat up a little straighter. "And I'm tired of flagging down cabs every time I want to leave the house. It would be nice to have a driver again."

"You won't even be living here," Lady Ashton said, giving her eldest daughter a warning look.

"George was a good man," Lord Ashton said thoughtfully. Lady Ashton turned to him, mouth open in surprise.

"Are you considering this, dear?"

He shrugged. "Perhaps. It would be nice to have someone we know we can trust. Perhaps, we fired him a little hastily."

I tried to hide my shock. Lord Ashton had always been the colder one of the two. He let his wife navigate the world with her bleeding heart and frequent hugs while he focused on the practicalities. But now, he was my best chance at helping George find a new job once I left the city.

"I've already spoken to George, and he would love to come back," I said. This was only half true. I'd spoken to George about finding him another position. I had not mentioned it would be with the previous employers who had let him go. However, George didn't seem the type to hold a grudge, so I didn't think he would mind.

"See?" Lord Ashton said, shrugging. "It seems settled to me. We need a driver and George is a good one."

Lady Ashton rolled her eyes and shrugged. "Fine. But we still can't take in the boy."

Lord Ashton nodded in agreement. "Yes, we have no space for the boy."

I jumped up and hugged them both, eliciting startled, but not altogether displeased hugs in return. "You have already done so much. Thank you. I'll give George the good news."

～

"WHAT ABOUT ASEEM?" George asked when I told him about his new position with Lord and Lady Ashton. He hadn't even paused to celebrate his own success before worrying over Aseem.

I turned to Aseem who was standing quietly in the corner, arms folded behind his back. Sometimes, because of how maturely he carried himself, it was easy to forget how young Aseem was. He had grown much taller in the short time we'd been in London, but he still had a roundness to his cheeks that gave away his young age.

"There wasn't a position open for you at the Beckingham's home, but I have other connections in the city," I assured him.

"You have already done enough for me, Miss Rose," he said, smiling. "I can't ask any more of you."

"And you do not have to ask me, Aseem. I will not see you deserted on the streets while I am away. You will have a job and a home. It is the very least you deserve after everything you have done for me."

He said nothing in response, but I noticed his eyes going glassy, and I turned away to give him his privacy.

Later that night, I sat down at my desk and penned a letter to the people who had been there for me since the beginning of my journey as Rose Beckingham.

DEAR MR. AND MRS. WORTHING,

. . .

I HOPE you will forgive me for how long it has been since I've written you. I know I promised to stay in touch, but as you know, life has been far from uneventful in my corner of the world. The last time we saw each other, the weekend in the country dissolved into murder, and I'm ashamed I haven't met with you since. I hope all has been well.

YOU'D BE PLEASED to know I solved a recent art theft. I haven't told many people about the case as it was intended to be a secret, but I know how much you believe in my detection skills, and I thought you'd enjoy being proven right.

I WOULD ALSO like you to be one of the first to know that I will be leaving London. I am incredibly sad to go, but duty to my family is propelling me forward. My cousins, Catherine and Alice, both of whom you met in Somerset, are going to New York City to escape the disruption their brother's crimes and murder have caused their lives here in London. My aunt, Lady Ashton, has asked me to accompany them. I am going simply to be a friendly face in a new city. I doubt I will be much help aside from that.

NOW, to the letter's purpose. (I know, I wish I could say this letter was written out of desire and not necessity, but does it make you feel better if I say it was written out of both?) Leaving the city means leaving the home I have created for myself here, including the people I employed to help me keep it. I have found a place for my driver with the Beckinghams, but they were unable to take in a young boy by the name of Aseem, and as I'm sure you can already guess, I'm writing to see if the two of you would have a place in your home and hearts for him?

. . .

HE IS THIRTEEN-YEARS-OLD—NEARLY *fourteen*—but *mature well beyond his years, quiet as a church mouse, and more loyal than anyone I've ever met. He would be a wonderful addition to your home, and I know you would not regret taking him in.*

I'M NOT *sure when I will be returning to London, so I'd like to stress that this situation wouldn't necessarily be temporary. But again, you will do no better than Aseem. He will work hard and win your hearts as he has won mine.*

PLEASE WRITE BACK SOON *with your decision. I do not wish to rush you, but I leave for New York City in two days. I only hope the journey to New York will be much less exciting than our own from Bombay to London. Still, I am glad it gave me time to get to know the two of you. I'm grateful for your friendship in my life. (I'm not trying to sweet talk you into accepting Aseem, but if my words have that effect, then they will have served two purposes.)*

LOVE,
    Rose Beckingham

I RECEIVED a response the next afternoon.

DEAR ROSE,

. . .

OF COURSE, *we will take in the boy, no sweet talk required. Mr. Worthing and I are not as young as we once were and had already been considering searching for extra help.*

OTHERWISE, *your letter was a disgrace. Much too short. I must have more details about the art theft and how you solved it. Also, I've been keeping up with the story of Edward Beckingham in the papers, but you must tell me how much of what I've read is true and how much is fiction.*

LONDON WILL MISS YOU. *Write soon!*

LOVE,
     Mrs. Worthing

21

————

My house looked much like it had when I'd first walked through it prior to my purchase. The furniture was covered in white cloths, windows pulled tight, fireplaces closed and sealed. Every room felt larger and every noise echoed off the wood-paneled walls. It was a sad sight. Much sadder than I'd anticipated.

Though London had not been at all what I'd expected, I had come to enjoy my time in the city. The Beckinghams had been a welcoming family, and George and Aseem filled what would have been a quiet house with living noise. It was always a comfort to lie in bed and hear their footsteps on the hallway below or a door opening and closing. I would miss them in New York.

"Are you ready, Miss Rose?" George asked, standing in the hallway between the dining room and sitting room. I'd told him he could move his things to Ashton House, but he refused to until I had officially left the city.

"Is my trunk in the car?" I asked.

He nodded and then his mouth twisted to the side. "It

wasn't so long ago that I was picking you up from the docks."

I smiled at him and then took one last look at the room. I smoothed down my burgundy top and gray wool skirt. My fingers itched for something else to pack or prepare, but the preparations were made. It was time to leave. "Time certainly has flown."

Lady Ashton had arranged for Catherine, Alice, and I to stay with an aunt in New York. Alice was anxious to leave, hardly sleeping in the days before we set sail, but I knew she would be homesick once we arrived.

"Kate Oliver went away to boarding school when she was twelve, and only comes back in the summers. She has always thought she was better than me, but how much better will it be that I get to live in a whole other country? She will absolutely die of jealousy."

Alice seemed to have turned into a typical adolescent overnight, and I worried what that would mean for myself and Catherine. We were barely adults ourselves, and I wondered everyday how Lady Ashton could trust us to manage her youngest daughter.

Catherine kept whatever enthusiasm she may have felt to herself. She busied herself with preparations and did her best to contain Alice's excitement.

"We are leaving because our brother has died," she whispered harshly to Alice one night after dinner. Lord and Lady Ashton had already retired to the sitting room, and Alice had rambled on through half the meal about the things she was excited to see in New York City.

Alice glared at her. "I know that. It does not mean I cannot be excited about things. Edward would have understood."

Then, she stomped off into the next room and continued the conversation where she had left off.

Adding onto my long list of concerns, I worried what would happen when Alice finally came to terms with her brother's death. She had taken to pretending as if nothing was different, reminiscing about Edward frequently, not at all bothered that it turned her father's face white as a sheet and made her mother hide her crying eyes behind her dinner napkin. Clearly, she hadn't accepted the reality that he was gone, and when she did, I was concerned it would hit her especially hard.

Otherwise, living in New York would be no different than London for me. I had known almost no one when I'd first come to London—not even the people who were supposed to be my family. Yet, I had made a life for myself. I knew I would do the same in New York. And this time, I would have Catherine and Alice. However, as our ship's departure grew nearer and nearer, I did not feel anxious or nervous to leave. There was simply a sadness. And while I tried to sort through my strange emotions, one person refused to leave my mind: Achilles Prideaux.

He had made me a grand offer to travel with him as a partner in his business, and I had never given him a response. Not really, anyway. I tried to write several letters to explain myself, but they ended up as ash in the fireplace. I had taken a long walk the afternoon before my ship was set to leave, hoping the right words would come to me when I saw him, but every time I neared his home, I would take a sharp turn and venture in another direction. I couldn't bring myself to face him again. Not after what he'd said.

He was fond of me. Much more so than I probably deserved after how long I had lied to him. And I didn't know what to do with that information. I knew how to talk to

Achilles, my friend. I did not know how to talk to Achilles, my potential suitor. So, in the end, I decided not to say good-bye. It was probably better that way, I told myself. I had tried to say goodbye to him on several occasions, and each one was worse than the last. One more attempt would only serve to embarrass us both and ruin whatever remained of the friendship we once shared.

The buildings outside the window became increasingly more industrial as the car neared the edge of town. The sky had been bright blue that morning, but as the day wore on, gray clouds gathered in heavy clusters, threatening to release a downpour at any moment. Catherine and Alice would be waiting for me near the ship, Lord and Lady Ashton there as well to wave goodbye. I wondered if it would be raining in New York too.

"I'll wave until the ship disappears into the horizon," Lady Ashton had said a few nights before.

"That could take hours," Catherine said. "It will be after midnight before you get home. Besides, we won't be able to see you. The ship will be too tall."

"How do you know? You've never been on a ship," Alice smarted.

"Neither have you," Catherine snapped back.

I wondered whether they would still wave if it were rain-ing, or if they would leave once we had walked up the gangplank.

I also wondered whether Achilles would come to say goodbye.

I knew it was silly to wonder such a thing. Of course, he wouldn't. Why would he? I hadn't told him when or from where the ship was leaving, though as a detective, I knew he was more than capable of finding that kind of information out. But even more than that, I had snubbed his advances and hurt his pride. Whatever opportunity had been there for me was likely gone.

He had offered me a way out of my lie. I could reclaim my true identity, explore the world as myself, no longer being forced to lie about my past. I could reminisce about my childhood, talk about my time spent in an orphanage, and finally, after months of lies, talk to someone about my dear friend Rose.

In many ways, not being able to talk about Rose had been the hardest part of becoming her. For ten years, she had been one of my dearest friends, and she had died. That was no small loss. Yet, I could tell no one of my grief. I couldn't visit her grave because it did not exist. I worried constantly that not talking about her would cause me to forget. Would I one day forget what she'd looked like? Would I forget how she had laughed with her whole body? How she would grab my hand and spin me around her bedroom any time I was being boring, and she thought I needed to be less serious?

I also feared I would forget myself. My parents had been murdered when I was a little girl and my brother had disappeared immediately afterward, reappearing only to be lost to me once again. I had so few memories of them left and being forced to repress them made them harder to recall. One day, I worried I wouldn't be able to at all. Where my family had once resided in my mind and heart would be an empty space.

I would be the first to admit that life as Rose Beckingham had become comfortable. Not only did I have a family who loved me, but I had enough money to live comfortably. People waited upon me and respected me simply because of my family connections. Nellie Dennet didn't have access to any of that. However, Nellie Dennet didn't have to lie.

Boarding the ship with Catherine and Alice and disembarking in New York would be locking myself into life as Rose Beckingham. It was a life of ease and luxury, yes, but also a life of deception. My existence had become a house of cards that even the slightest wind could topple. Though I had tried to deny Achilles's words, he had been right. It was only a matter of time before I slipped up and someone caught me out.

The city was fading away behind us, and George was calmly driving, unaware of my anguish in the backseat. Was I making the right choice? Did I realistically have another option?

Achilles had asked me to join him in Morocco as myself. I could drop the pretense of Rose Beckingham and reclaim Nellie Dennet. I wouldn't have to spend every conversation worried that my accent would falter or that the people around me would notice my lack of high society manners. I could be perfectly myself.

Even the thought of that felt foreign. What would it be like to feel completely at ease around a group of strangers? To be confident in my own skin? To not hide and lie about my past and my experiences?

And even more, what would it be like to be with Achilles Prideaux? He had been a highlight of my time in London— a friend when I needed one. But now he was offering the opportunity to travel to exotic locations and assist him in his investigations. And more than that, it was the opportunity for our friendship to grow and possibly blossom into something sweeter. Something that terrified me, but that I wanted all the same.

I sat in the backseat and weighed the options before me, trying to decide who I wanted to be and how I wanted to navigate life. Did I want to be financially comfortable or emotionally comfortable? Did I want to live a lie, constantly afraid of being caught? Or, did I want to tell the truth on my own terms and create my own future?

New York was the promise of grandeur, but Morocco was the promise of a fresh start.

Catherine had been right. I spent so much of my time worrying about everyone else, trying to make sure everyone was taken care of. I had come to London in the first place to find Jimmy and offer him the help I believed he had asked for. But that mystery had been solved, so why was I still pretending to be Rose? To keep the Beckinghams from enduring any more pain? To keep their names out of the papers? To ensure everyone else except for myself was comfortable and well taken care of?

I realized now that I couldn't think about anyone else. Not Catherine or Alice. Not Lord or Lady Ashton. Not George or Aseem. Not Achilles Prideaux. I had to be selfish. I had to think about myself. What would lead to the happiest life for me?

The answer popped into my head in a second, just as it had repeatedly in the preceding days. My mind was made up. I knew what I wanted.

22

I could never get over how far-reaching the ocean was. I liked to imagine the many different shores the water washed up on. How many different people were splashing in the foamy water along the sand, not realizing how connected they all were. The same water that lapped against the sides of the ship I was on was, at the same time, touching different continents.

I leaned forward against the railing, my hands gripping the cool metal, and looked straight down. The water was a deep navy, but as I looked out towards the horizon, it lightened and shifted until it was a pale white shimmer in the distance, brushing against the shore of my new temporary home.

The world looked different from the water. Low-hanging clouds hung in a haze and cast everything in silver. The sun reflected off the few windows of glass, blinding me even though we were still miles out. We'd been at sea for five days, going on six, and I was anxious to touch dry land again. I was also anxious to be in the city. I had been hearing about it for days, and I couldn't wait to see it for myself.

"We are nearly there."

I turned to see Achilles standing behind me, the sea wind mussing his usually well-oiled hair. Spending days on end with him made me realize that he wasn't always immaculately groomed. Though, no matter how many hints I made, he refused to shave his mustache, and he always managed to keep the thin strip of hair above his lip combed and shiny.

"Are you regretting your offer yet?" I asked, resting my elbows on the railing. "Because I'm sure I can catch the next ship home if you are."

"And where would home be?" he asked, tilting his head to the side, a smile on his lips.

"I'd find somewhere," I said with an easy shrug. "Maybe Spain or Australia."

"Not London?"

I shook my head. "No, I think I'm done with London. For a while, at least. It would probably be best to let everything settle down there before I return."

My smile faltered for only a moment, but Achilles saw it.

"They will forgive you," he said, taking a step towards me.

"Would you forgive me if I had run away from you without a word of explanation or even a goodbye?" I asked, looking up at him. "Honestly?"

He thought about it for a long moment, and I appreciated that about Achilles. He never said what I wanted to hear simply because he knew I wanted to hear it. I could always count on getting the truth from him. "I'm not sure."

I looked down at my shoes, scuffing one black toe along the wooden deck.

"But," he said, leaning forward to catch my eye, drawing my face upward. "I still don't think you should be sad."

"And why is that?" I asked.

"Because you loved the Beckinghams. Rose and her parents. Lord and Lady Ashton and their children. Knowing them brought great joy to your life."

"And great sadness," I added, thinking also of the disappointment I must have brought to their lives with the letter I'd sent from our last port. It would have arrived by now, and I wondered every day whether I'd ever receive a response.

"I've found the two often go hand in hand. It seems impossible to have one without the other," Achilles said thoughtfully. "So, I stand by my statement. You should not be sad. You and the Beckinghams brought one another great joy, and I believe that overrides the sadness."

I didn't know if or when I would ever feel the way Achilles did about my situation, but I liked to think I would get there one day. I wanted to know the Beckinghams. I wanted to see Alice mature into adulthood and watch Lady Ashton become a grandmother. I wanted to receive letters full of gossip from Mrs. Worthing. I didn't want to let the life I'd found as Rose Beckingham fade away completely. After all, it was that life that brought me to Achilles Prideaux.

Maybe that was why I had left the door open. I hadn't completely severed my pretense of being Rose, but had only written vaguely in my letter that I needed a new life and time away—indefinitely. I hoped Catherine and Alice could manage in New York without me. I had entrusted full control of my fortune to my uncle and underlined my willingness to sign paperwork to that effect. With any luck, that would right the family fortunes, even if it did leave me more or less penniless.

Achilles moved to stand next to me, and we both watched in silence as we sailed into the Strait of Gibraltar. Other passengers who had been below deck began making their way up, finding spots at the rails, everyone wanting a view of the harbor of Tangiers. And now that I was seeing it for myself, I understood why.

The city was a beautiful tapestry of its history. Spires and minarets twisted towards the impossibly blue sky, towering over an eclectic sprawl of mud brick homes, stark white palaces, and intricately decorated mosques. All of this surrounded by a forest of green olive trees.

"It's beautiful," I said in a reverent whisper.

"Wait until you are walking the streets," Achilles said with a smile. "You will love it."

"Don't we have work to do?" I asked. "We are here to solve a case of espionage, correct?"

"Yes, but there is always time to appreciate the beauty around us." He turned to me and winked, and my cheeks instantly flushed.

I looked back to the harbor, watching as more of the city came into view, and reached to my neck for the locket that still hung there. For so long, the locket had been a reminder of the life I'd left behind in New York and the family I'd lost. But now, the small scrap of paper I'd carried with me for so many years was gone. Instead, I left the gold locket empty as a promise to myself that one day, whether soon or far into the future, I would find something worthy of holding there again.

My life was not over, it was just beginning, and I intended to live it well.

ABOUT THE AUTHOR

Blythe Baker is a thirty-something bottle redhead from the South Central part of the country. When she's not slinging words and creating new worlds and characters, she's acting as chauffeur to her children and head groomer to her household of beloved pets.

Blythe enjoys long walks with her dog on sweaty days, grubbing in her flower garden, cooking, and ruthlessly de-cluttering her overcrowded home. She also likes binge-watching mystery shows on TV and burying herself in books about murder.

To learn more about Blythe, visit her website and sign up for her newsletter at www.blythebaker.com

Made in the USA
San Bernardino, CA
28 April 2020